Disney
HOCUS POCUS

Disney HOCUS POCUS

WRITTEN BY A. W. JANTHA

BASED ON THE SCREENPLAY BY
MICK GARRIS & NEIL CUTHBERT

STORY BY
DAVIS KIRSCHNER & MICK GARRIS

ILLUSTRATED BY GRIS GRIMLY

DISNEY PRESS
LOS ANGELES   NEW YORK

First Hardcover Edition, August 2022

1 3 5 7 9 10 8 6 4 2

FAC-034274-22176

Printed in the United States of America

This book is set in 1786 GLC Fournier and Truesdell Pro

Library of Congress Control Number: 2022931907

ISBN 978-1-368-07668-5

Reinforced binding

For more Disney Press fun, visit www.disneybooks.com.

Cover and interior designed by Scott Piehl

On All Hallows' Eve,
when the moon is round,
a virgin will summon us from
under the ground.

We Shall Be Back!
and the lives of all the children
of salem shall be mine!

—Winifred Sanderson
October 31, 1693
*Last words, as recorded
in the journal of Samuel Parris*

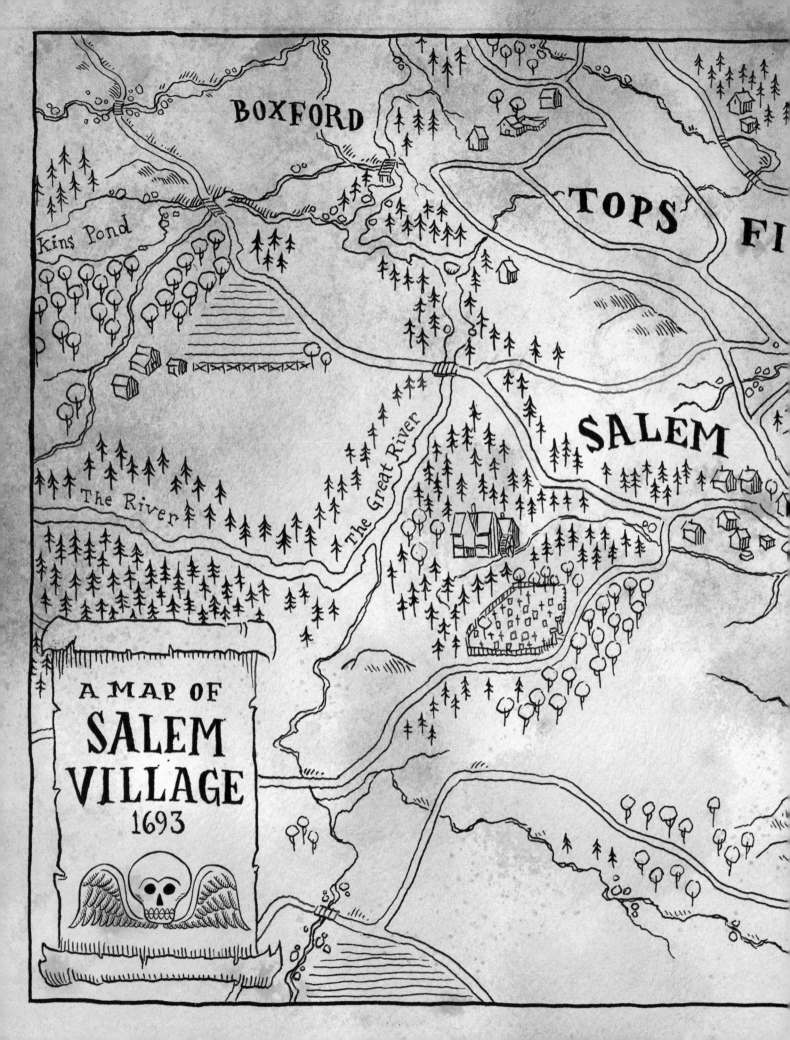

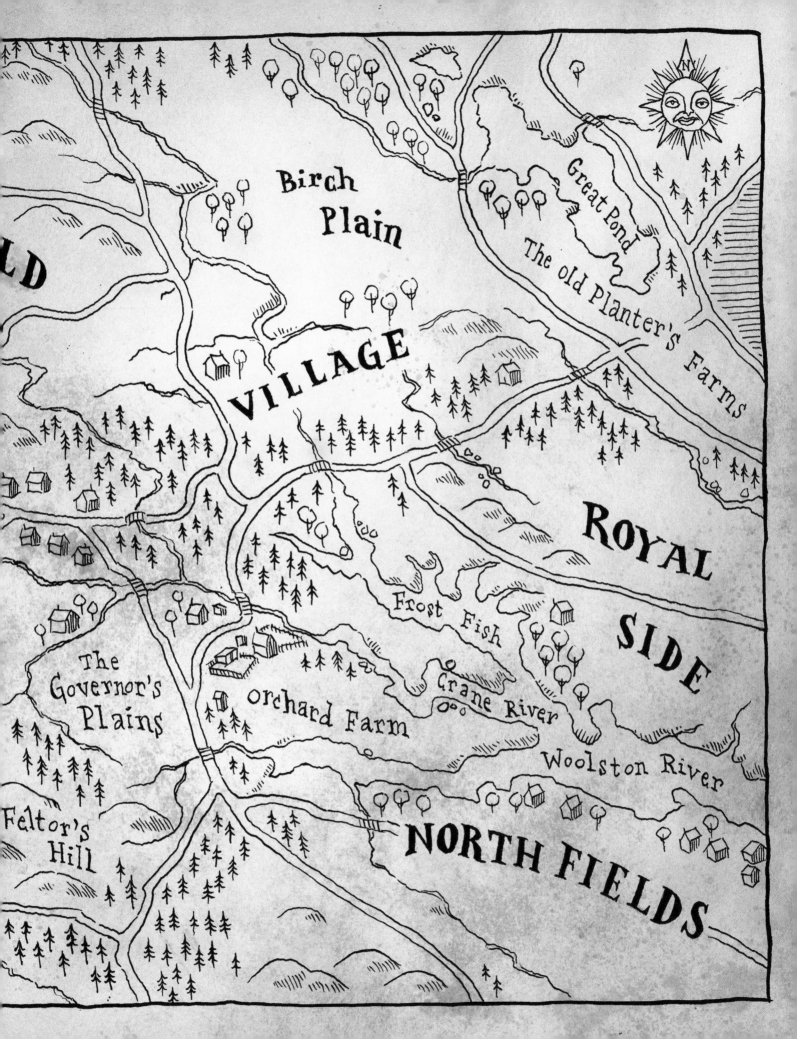

Disney

Hocus Pocus

PROLOGUE

SALEM, 1693

 HE WORLD was full of wild things then. It brimmed with oak and hemlock and dark whispering places that turned you round and round until there was no turning back.

The womenfolk said that on early mornings near the harbor you could hear echoes of witchsong, which sounded like birdsong but more bitter. The menfolk said godliness would save them from any witches, but they honed their axes and twisted new rope just the same.

The witches said there was nothing so sweet as the shinbones of little girls. Or perhaps a well-braised scapula with sparrow spleen compote. It was all in the preparation.

They lived near town, the witches, but not so near as to be a bother, until a milk cow died or a child took sick. Then the town would start to mutter about the Sanderson girls—Mary and Sarah and especially Winnie—who had not been girls for a very long time but who did not merit the title "ladies."

Someone always intervened.

They're no bother, someone would say. *Just batty girls playing in the woods.*

Leave them be, someone would say. *Don't you remember how kind their mother was, and how generous?*

It all made perfect sense at the time, but once the people of Salem left the town meeting and went back to work, not a one of them could remember who that someone had been.

That is, until Emily went missing. It was not unlike Emily Binx to stray so close to the wood. Her mother had often scolded her for doing precisely that, though she tried not to scold too hard, for nine-year-old Emily was a serious child, and pious, paging through her prayer book without minding where her footsteps took her.

Emily was old enough to know the rumors about the Sanderson sisters, but she also knew that whenever she ran across any of them in town, they were kind to her. It was rare to see Miss Winnie or Miss Mary or Miss Sarah smile, what with their crooked backs and twisted, dusty faces, but when they noticed her, they beamed and clapped—well, Mary and Sarah, anyway—and praised her pink cheeks and pretty hands. Her mother never praised those things, for fear of encouraging vanity and sin. Even skeptical Miss Winnie would pat Emily's shoulder awkwardly and tease that she should return to her mother lest Winnie eat the little girl right up.

All this to say that Emily was not afraid of the wood as others were, and was especially less afraid than her brother, Thackery, who, like his best friend, Elijah, was seven years older than Emily and of an age when boys found anything at all to do with girls or women highly suspect.

So when the wood began to creep into her dreams, it didn't startle Emily.

In the dreams, the field between Salem and the trees smelled of warm hay and fresh flowers, and its waves of trailing sweet-grass tickled her arms and legs as she walked.

In the dreams, the edge of the field ran right up to the edge of the wood and then stopped, as if perplexed about where to go next.

In the dreams, the wood was cool and welcoming, and the air tasted faintly of damp soil and crumbling bark—a taste that seemed as sweet as almond cake to young Emily, for it promised an adventure to rival her well-worn copy of *Pilgrim's Progress*.

Thackery had begun to dream of that place, too—that knife's edge between the world he knew and the world of witches—but his dreams were thick with moss-colored smoke and the press of hands upon his skin and the taste of sweat and bile and river muck. The dreams made him wake, night after night, more tired than the day before, but he didn't tell his parents or his sister or even Elijah, for he feared the dreams meant something dark about his mind—or worse, about his heart.

Emily didn't tell because she was afraid her mother might scold her for letting her imagination run beyond the pages of her prayer book.

And the other children didn't tell for their own reasons, each of them more personal than the next.

When Emily Binx woke to the dreamy light of dawn, she first believed it was due to the cocks crowing in the yard—but for whatever reason, the animals weren't making a single sound.

Emily crept to the window and found the roosters asleep— even the chickens, who clucked softly as they dozed. It was so strange that she slipped out of the house without changing from her bedclothes, an act that would surely scandalize her mother if she caught her.

There was a soft song in the air that sounded nothing like birds, but also not quite like the hymns the pastor's wife led at church. It sounded more like the delicate crust on sugared almonds or the sweet cream of Christmas custard. It sounded like something that could melt or sour if it wasn't used up right away.

Emily stepped into the yard and past the clustered chickens and nodding family of sheep whose coats were thickening for winter. She petted the nose of Mopsie, the black pony her father had brought back from last year's trip to Boston, and giggled when he released a happy little snort.

She passed the milliner's house, and the butcher's, but their curtains were drawn and their houses stood silent. A downy rabbit was napping in the yard of the town's best baker, as if it had settled down to sleep in the open—unafraid of hungry foxes or rowdy boys with sticks. Elizabeth, the baker herself, was awake, though. There was a smell of boiling fruit and sugar, and Emily spotted her through the shutters of her kitchen window, humming to herself.

Elizabeth lived in a small cottage on the edge of town with her husband and daughter, though they were scarcely seen since the witch trials had begun in Salem. Those who did see her when she dropped off baked goods remarked on her simple beauty. She was a tall woman in her early twenties, with dark curly hair, and she wore her pale yellow cloak in almost any weather.

A little girl around Emily's age peeped her head just above the sill. The girl had clear chestnut eyes and a chipper smile, and she gave Emily a friendly wave.

"Ismay, get away from the windows," came a man's voice from within the house, hushed and urgent.

The little girl ducked away.

Elizabeth stepped up to the open window and locked eyes with Emily. "What brings you outside so early this morning, Miss Emily?" Elizabeth inquired, pushing the window open to better see the girl. "And how on earth did your mother let you outside without shoes, my dear?"

Emily giggled. "The whole world seems to be asleep."

"John Barker's ale must have been strong last night," said Elizabeth. She held up the apple she was slicing. "I'll have pie later, but you won't be allowed in until you've changed."

Emily nodded somberly. "I'm going to find the music first," she said.

Elizabeth's demeanor turned suddenly grave. "Don't follow it," she warned.

"But it's prettier than any tune I've ever heard before, miss," said Emily.

"Beautiful things have a way of obscuring danger, my dear girl. Don't—" She stopped short as the smell of burning fruit filled the air and the sound of clumsy gurgling reached her ears. She hastened to remove the delicate preserve from the stove, but when she returned to the window a moment later, Emily was already gone.

Thackery jolted awake to the sound of Mopsie whinnying like he'd been kicked.

He sat up straight, a layer of sweat sticking his pale linen shirt to his back, and let his ears adjust to the commotion outside the window. The sun was high—he must have slept through the cock crow, which meant his father would be angry because he hadn't yet milked the cow. Thackery flopped back into bed, wondering whether he could plead sick. He glanced to his left, hoping he could ask Emily to cover for him, but her bed was empty and unmade. Her church dress still hung by the fire, as did her gabled cap.

Thackery hurried out of bed and looked about the small plain bedroom they shared at the back of the house. Emily's shoes were by the door, which was very unlike her.

He sniffed the air but couldn't catch the smell of woodsmoke that would mean his mother was preparing porridge in the main part of the house. Nor could he hear the good-natured sound of his father greeting neighbors as they passed on their way back from the harbor.

Something wasn't right.

He dashed into the yard, where the chickens were scrambling as if they knew it was time for supper. Mopsie had torn himself from the tree, and his lead hung limp and ominous from an upper branch. A shiver crept down Thackery's spine. From the gate of the sheep's pen, Thackery spotted Elijah Morris, his best friend, who was rubbing his eyes as if he'd just risen, as well.

"Elijah!" he called, forgetting his own shoes as he crossed between their yards.

When Thackery grabbed Elijah's forearm, his friend turned to him, blinking as if coming out of a dream. Elijah was only a hair's width taller than Thackery—at least, that's what Thackery said—and wore an identical linen shirt and long-locked hairstyle. The townsfolk called the two of them accidental twins.

"Has thee seen my sister, Emily?" asked Thackery.

"Nay," said Elijah. "But look: they conjure."

Thackery followed his friend's gaze and saw, far past the fields that surrounded town and deep within the Salem Wood, a plume of heavy smoke crawling into the clear late-morning sky. It was an unnatural shade of pink—bright and conspicuous. It made his stomach turn.

"The woods," Thackery managed, the half-dreamed ghost of witchy hands tightening around his neck. He grabbed Elijah by the shirtsleeve, and together they raced down the lane and to the field. There Thackery caught sight of his sister's slight frame slipping into the shadow of the trees.

"Wake my father," he told Elijah, keeping his eyes trained on where his sister had just been. "Summon the others. Go!"

Before Elijah could answer, Thackery was racing toward the witching wood, shouting his sister's name. He leaped over one branch and ducked beneath another, and then lost his footing and tumbled down the steep embankment until he landed in a thick bed of browned leaves. He groaned, forcing himself up onto one arm and then farther up onto his hurting bare feet.

Before him stood the Sanderson house, a cottage that sat crookedly upon its haunches and sagged in its eaves despite being younger than many buildings in Salem proper. Intricate wooden shutters obscured its windows, and weeds grew in thick drifts around the house and even between some of the floorboards of the porch. A few sported bright blue flowers despite the chill of October's last day. Thackery had no doubt that these blossoms smelled and tasted like honey but would kill a man within a few minutes.

On the house's left side, a huge waterwheel caught the tiny creek and turned, groaning from the labor. Above it, the smoke hung thick and promised something as wicked as a snake in paradise.

Emily disappeared inside as Thackery watched, helpless—trapped by a memory of clambering down there with Elijah when

both of them were twelve, of daring each other to throw pebbles at the door, of his heart knocking hard against his chest when the door opened and Winifred Sanderson stepped out with her wild red hair and threatened to roast them with chicken of the woods and worm snakes' tongues.

Thackery pushed aside his memories and crossed the flat stepping stones to a low window that looked into the only room of the house. Inside, the sisters were doing the Devil's work, each of them wearing a heavy cape with a pointed hood—one green as leaves before the fall, one red as clay, and one a purple deeper than an elderberry's juice. Together, the women danced and rocked slowly around his poor sweet sister. They had seated Emily in a heavy-looking chair, and she looked patiently up at them as if she expected a present at the end of it all. Her eyes widened when she saw Thackery, and he hurried out of sight and shut the window.

He wasted no time clambering past the waterwheel and ducking into an alcove just as the creak of a rusted hinge pierced the air. The high haughty voice of Winifred Sanderson rang out above him.

"Oh, look," she sighed. "Another glorious morning. Makes me sick!"

The window slammed shut again, and Thackery leaned into the stone of the old building.

He was relieved not to have been caught, but it didn't help

the feeling that his ribs were knotted tight with rope. Emily was trapped inside with the witches, and he had no idea what to do.

"My darling," crooned Winifred Sanderson, and Thackery was sure the words were meant for Emily.

But then she added, equally lovingly, "My little book. We must continue with our spell now that our little guest of honor has arrived. Wake up," she coaxed, like a mother to her child. "Wake up, darling. Yes—oh, come along. There you are."

Thackery clambered up the waterwheel, which allowed him to enter the house through a thick-paned window on the second floor. It opened to a narrow loft that looked down into the large room, which made it the perfect hiding spot. Thackery slunk in and pressed himself as close to the floorboards as he could manage, peering down at his sister and the witches below.

"Ah, there it is," Winifred was saying. Her book was open on an angled table, and a massive iron pot was bubbling over an open fire beside her. She read from the book's pages: " 'Bring to a full rolling bubble; add two drops of oil of boil. Mix blood of owl with the herb that's red. Turn three times, pluck a hair from my head. Add a dash of pox and a dead man's toe.' " She turned to Sarah, the narrowest sister, and perhaps the youngest, though no one in Salem seemed to remember. "Dead man's toe," Winifred ordered. "And make it a fresh one."

Sarah Sanderson brightened then and began to dance around

chorusing the command, and Thackery cringed. He thought of George Flamsteed, the kind old fisherman whose boat had capsized in late September. He'd washed ashore untouched—except that he'd been missing both of his big toes. For days after, the townsfolk had whispered about the Devil's work.

Mary tossed a toe into the pot and then flung another one at Sarah for good measure.

When a wayward digit landed upon Winifred's back, she rounded on them both. "Will you two *stop* that?" she demanded. "I need to concentrate." She turned back to her book and then, satisfied, called her sisters to the pot. The surface of the bubbling liquid was obscured by a thick sheet of white smoke.

As Thackery spied, he chewed his bottom lip, tasting blood. Emily sat quietly off to the side, and he wondered what could possibly be going through her head. He'd seen a flash of recognition from her before, but now she sat as serenely as the doll he'd believed her to be when the midwife had first wrapped her in a clean blanket.

"'One thing more and all is done,'" chanted Winifred, waving her hands over the surface of the pot, "'add a bit of thine own tongue.'"

At once, all three sisters stuck out their tongues and bit down with a crunch, turning Thackery's stomach. They spat into the pot and began to stir the vile liquid with a large wooden spoon.

"One drop of this," breathed Winifred, "and her life will be mine." She caught herself. "I mean, *ours*."

Thackery looked over his shoulder, but there wasn't a single sound outside. Where was Elijah? Where was his father? Surely they'd arrive at any moment.

When the sisters began to advance on Emily, Winifred carrying the huge spoon of the dark bubbling potion, Thackery jumped up. "No!" he shouted, leaping down from the loft before they could feed any of their wicked brew to his sister.

"A *boy*," growled Winifred. "Get him, you fools!"

Thackery dodged the two younger witches, dancing around the bubbling pot so they couldn't catch him. He grabbed the lip of the pot and shoved, not caring about the searing pain that shot through his hands.

Once the poison was spilled across the ground, he rushed toward his sister, but it was too late: Winifred had given her the draught of potion left in that huge wooden spoon. The decrepit witch delicately—even lovingly—wiped his sister's mouth with her own cloak before turning to face him.

"Always keep your eyes on the prize, my boy!" She cackled as she raised her free hand. The air filled with a violent green light.

All at once, Thackery's world filled up and spilled over with hurt.

His muscles betrayed him, his field of vision blurred and went dark, and his body collapsed like a bundle of sticks on the floor.

Thackery's mind went blank from the pain in his body. When he could finally blink again, he wasn't sure whether he'd lost a few seconds or a few minutes or much, much longer. He tipped his head to the side and saw that Emily was still there, as were the three hideous Sanderson sisters.

Emily sat serenely in the wooden chair, attentive but church-quiet. Her pale skin and white sleep dress looked almost iridescent in the house's low light. Thackery watched, helpless, as that iridescence turned into a warm golden glow the likes of which one might expect to see spill from the skin of an angel.

" 'Tis her life force!" said Winifred. "The potion works." She stretched her arms toward her sisters. "Take my hands—we will share her."

Fingers entwined, the three witches advanced upon Emily. They leaned forward and inhaled deeply. Curls of amber light drifted away from Emily and down their wretched throats.

Thackery dragged himself to a nearby ladder and managed to prop himself up, but the world sloshed around him and he couldn't think of how words were supposed to be strung together. He watched his sister, though, and felt that his heart would break.

The sisters took a final inhale and the light around Emily disappeared behind their lips. Emily's narrow chin tipped forward and her body went limp. Her face was suddenly drawn and sallow, her skin threaded with thin gray veins as if her blood, too, had been stolen from her.

Thackery lurched toward her but only managed to vomit onto the floor. He tried to look away from his sister, but he couldn't help staring at her in horror. Emily. Dead. Dead and shrunken like a frail old woman. Thackery vomited again. He hadn't eaten since supper, and the thin bile from his stomach soured his tongue.

Sarah Sanderson spun about, running fingers through her newly golden curly hair. "I am beautiful!" she squealed. "Boys will love me!"

Mary's plump face looked nearly pleasant, thanks to the color creeping back into her cheeks. She pouted her red lips, which still twisted to one side. "We're young!" she laughed, clapping.

Winifred hurried to pick up a mirror. Her face fell, and for a moment Thackery suspected she wished she hadn't been so generous in sharing with her sisters. "Well," she said, "younger." Then a surge of energy seemed to ripple through her, and she raised both arms in triumph. "But it's a start!" She cackled.

The sisters promenaded together while Thackery continued to drag himself onto unsteady feet.

"Oh, Winifred," cooed Mary, "thou art a mere sprig of a girl."

"Liar!" Winifred crowed. "But I shall be a sprig of a girl forever," she said, twirling each of her sisters, "once I suck the life out of all the children in Salem!" She turned to face Thackery and beamed, then advanced on him. "Let's brew another batch," she suggested.

"You hag," he growled. "There are not enough children in the *world* to make thee young and beautiful."

That made Winifred stop short. "Hag," she repeated distastefully. "Sisters, did you hear what he called you?"

Thackery wanted to point out that he'd been speaking specifically to her, but she spoke again before he could muster the energy: "Whatever shall we do with him?"

"Barbecue and fillet him," suggested Mary.

"Hang him on a hook," said Sarah, reaching for his chest, "and let me play with him."

"No," snapped Winifred, and then, more softly, she called for her book. The heavy tome floated through the air to reach her. The book was bound in scraps of thick, tanned human skin and roughly stitched together with thread that made the seams look like scars on a dead man's face. A metal clasp on the book's cover encircled a bit of puckered leather in the shape of an eye. "Dazzle me, my darling," she crooned. The book opened of its own accord, and she paged through it until she found the perfect spell. "His punishment shall not be to die, but to live forever with his *guilt*."

"As what, Winnie?" her sisters asked, delighted.

She stepped toward Thackery, and though he tried to evade her walnut-brown eyes and the sight of her large teeth and narrow

pursed lips, his ears filled with her chanting: "'Twist the bones and bend the back,'" she said, and her sisters murmured a soft spell beneath her words. Thackery winced, but Winifred went on: "'Trim him of his baby fat. Give him fur as black as black. Just . . . like . . . this.'"

Thackery felt his body twisting and turning in on itself, felt his bones snapping and reshaping into smaller, thinner versions of themselves. The last spell had felt like lightning beneath his skin, but this felt like a terrible bubbling in his marrow, and even as he screamed, he heard his voice come back in a shrill yowl.

The house rattled with the pounding of fists on its doors and windows, and through his pain, Thackery heard his father's voice. But it was too late.

He dragged himself to safety under a chest of drawers and let the pain sweep over his body and through his mind, spiriting his consciousness away.

The verdict was settled before the trial began, but the Sanderson witches' case was not helped by their refusal to show remorse.

That very same night—a dark, drizzling end to All Hallows' Eve—the three sisters stood on barrels stinking of fish, three lengths of rough rope looped around three guilty necks, and they cackled and teased the crowd as their sentences were read under the light of flickering lanterns and hungry-looking torches.

"They're mad," said the tray maker to the milliner. "When did they turn so mad?"

"When they sold their souls to the Devil in a despicable tryst with yellow hellfire and wickedness," said the milliner, as if he'd been there.

"Hmmm," mused the tray maker. "It seemed to help Sarah's complexion, though."

It began to rain then—fat drops that soaked woolen tunics and ran into well-worn boots. The judge—who was also the priest of Salem and two bordering townships and, in his humble opinion, severely overworked and underappreciated—tried to speed things along.

"What say thee, witches?" he demanded.

Sarah Sanderson tittered on her barrel. "We say thou weren't so judgy when coming to us last May for a potency potion. . . ." She cast her eyes below the man's round stomach and batted her lashes as the crowd broke into whispers and shifted from one soggy foot to the other.

"Lying jezebel!" cried the judge.

But before Sarah could retort, the father of dead Emily spoke up. "Winifred Sanderson," he said. "I will ask thee one final time: what hast thou done with my son, Thackery?"

"Thackery?" asked the eldest witch. In the dim torchlight, her face looked like chalk against the scarlet of her curls.

"Answer me!" he shouted. His arm was around the shoulders of his wife, who wept openly into his damp jacket.

"Well, I don't know!" Winifred protested, then gave her sisters a knowing, secret smile. "Cat's *got my tongue!*"

The Sanderson witches shrieked with laughter at Winifred's joke. As the sound of it died down, Sarah chafed at the rope around her neck. "This is terribly uncomfortable," she said.

Winifred cleared her throat, and before anyone in Salem could stop them, the Sanderson witches began to sing and chant in unison: *"Thrice I with mercury purify and spit upon the twelve tables."*

"Don't listen!" cried the judge. "Cover your ears!"

The gathered mass rushed to heed him as the sisters spat into the crowd.

"Don't drop the book!" someone shouted, but it was too late. Elijah Morris, the judge's apprentice and a boy who'd lost his best friend to these wicked sisters only that morning, covered his ears, too, dropping Winifred's leather-bound spell book as he did. The heavy thing sank into the mud with a satisfied squish. A moment later it flew open of its own accord, hundreds of pages shuddering and chuckling in the wind.

Mary and Sarah looked gleefully at it, the latter clapping her slender hands.

But Winifred, the eldest, let her gaze linger on the back of the crowd, her brown eyes piercing and gone almost black but her expression somehow bemused, like a cat who'd just transformed her master into a crippled mouse. Then her attention snapped back to her spell book. A laugh tumbled out of her broad chest. "Fools!" she crowed, relishing the word. "All of you! My ungodly book speaks to you: On All Hallows' Eve, when the moon is round, a virgin will summon us from under the ground." Her delight bubbled over into her sisters, who giggled and beamed alongside her. "We shall be back!" Winifred proclaimed. "And the lives of all the children of Salem shall be mine!"

White lightning cracked across the sky, and the executioner, dressed all in black, kicked down the barrels, Sarah, Winifred, and Mary dropping in quick succession. Their bodies shuddered and their toes stretched on swinging stockinged legs, and at last they were still and singing no more.

As the crowd began to shuffle off, the spell book was closed and lifted. As the book rose, the eyelid on its cover blinked open and the watery green iris searched out its rescuer.

Through a film of cataracts and rain, the spell book's eye saw thick dark curls obscuring a face, and then it was tucked beneath an arm and secreted away.

CHAPTER 1

SALEM, 1993

NOCK-KNOCKS," said Dani, grinning up at her sixteen-year-old brother as she trotted down the sidewalk. Leaves drifted through the air around them—thin slips of yellow and broad, shaggy orange things the size and shape of their dad's hands—and the morning was just starting to break open and turn the world gold.

Max rolled his eyes and swung his bike in a big loop to match her slow progress. "Can you please *not*?"

It was Halloween, and the houses on both sides of the little neighborhood street were decked out with cobwebs and tombstones, giant spiders and jack-o'-lanterns—some of which were already starting to sag a little with mold.

Dani giggled as she ran through the pale tendrils of a ghost horde gathered in a tree.

"Ta-tas," she said, a little louder. Her pointed black hat sported a thin orange trim around the brim, which matched her sun-patterned jacket and striped skirt. She'd dressed as a witch, but in her own words, "a fancy one." The grin she gave Max, though, was more impish than witchy.

Max glanced behind them to make sure the street was still as deserted as when they had left for school. "Seriously, Dani. Not the place."

He should've known better than to talk about Allison Watts to Jack, because Jack still lived in Santa Monica, and Max's house had a shared phone line and a nosy eight-year-old.

"YABOS," Dani squealed.

Max blushed hard, looking over his shoulder. "I'm going to leave you," he said. "Find your own way to school." He spun another loop, catching too much speed on the turn. He stopped short before hitting the curb.

Dani stopped, too, eyes sparkling with mischief beneath the brim of her witch's hat. A few strands of tawny hair stuck to her red lipstick. "Then Mom will ground you forever," she said.

"Maybe that wouldn't be so bad," he muttered.

Dani put a sympathetic hand on his shoulder. "Oh, don't

be that way," she said. "Then how will you ever see Allison's bazookas?"

Max groaned, leaning forward over his handlebars. "Please stop," he begged. "It's not even like that."

"It sounded a lot like that." She tugged on his sleeve to get them moving again.

Max relented, bike wobbling as he pedaled slowly beside his sister. "That's why you shouldn't eavesdrop on people," he said. "You lose context. One day you'll know what that means."

"Does it mean you saving up to run away to Jack's house and become the next X-Ray Glasses? Because I heard about that, too."

"The X-Ray Spex," Max muttered. "You know, I don't have to walk you to school anymore if I don't want to."

It was true: one of the few perks he'd been promised about their family's move from LA to Salem was that they'd live far enough from school that Dani would qualify for bus pickup. But the previous night she'd said the bus made her lonely, and she'd begged him to bike ahead and meet her one stop early so they could walk the rest of the way together. He'd agreed against his better judgment. She was still his little sister, after all, and as long as she'd been going to school, they'd been walking together. But now he was paying the price for nostalgia.

"But you do want to," said Dani, dancing through the

graveyard on someone's front lawn. "Or you would've said no." She stepped on a button, and a plastic corpse with matted black hair sat up with a shout, making her shriek and race back to the sidewalk.

As they rounded the corner, Max saw, at the top of the hill, the skinny blond and the no-necked bonehead known as Jay and Ernie. In the two weeks since his family had moved to Salem, Max had avoided any run-ins with the town bullies, but he could already tell they were the kind of boys whose kindergarten teachers, searching for something nice to say during parent–teacher conferences, would've settled on *persistent*.

Jay and Ernie's lackeys seemed to appear out of nowhere as they swaggered down the middle of the road, the embellishments on their faux-leather jackets glinting dully in the morning light.

"You know," said Max, wheeling around, "I think Mom told me they're handing out candy at the side entrance."

He felt bad about lying to Dani, but she'd get more than enough Airheads and Pixy Stix later.

"Hey!" she protested as they approached the annex door. "There's no candy—"

But her brother was already gone, speeding off toward Jacob Bailey High.

Max was kneeling beside his bike, tying his shoelace, when a shadow spilled over his shoulder and onto the grass.

He tensed, expecting Ernie's hot pickle breath to hit his shoulder any minute. To buy time, he undid his laces and tied them again, carefully. The pristine white toe and accents of the otherwise black Nikes started to blur as Max considered the best way to slip away unscathed. He wasn't about to let some mouth breather spit on his new sneakers just to get a rise out of him. He'd only gotten them as a pity gift from his parents when they'd announced their surprise move to The-Place-with-the-Witch-Trials, Massachusetts.

"You dressed up!"

Max turned to see Allison Watts smiling down at him. He glanced down at his shirt. A burst of tie-dye swirled up at him.

"I didn't, actually," he said.

Allison smirked. "Just that California lifestyle?"

Max grinned. He hated when other people made lame California jokes, but Allison earned a pass because she'd helped him find the chemistry lab on his first day—not that he expected her to remember that now. Allison was the kind of person who helped classmates with homework in the hallway before first period; who always waited the appropriate amount of time before answering teachers' questions, which turned her into a classroom hero instead of a show-off; and who had an intensity about her that made Max feel like he wanted to be part of her story. He could tell she'd become someone great one day—a president or an inventor or the CEO of a company that made flying cars. So when Allison cracked a joke about California, Max found that it made his stomach flip in a way that interfered with his ability to grimace.

He opened his mouth to introduce himself, but no sound emerged. That day, like the past three days, he thought about asking her out, but then he thought about her rejecting him and how he'd have to awkwardly extract himself from the situation, which made walking through town with his sister howling about bazookas sound like a fun weekend activity.

Allison watched his face, which must've been cycling through expressions of both hope and abject fear. When he still didn't speak, her smile softened. "Well," she said, "I'll see you around, California."

"Bye—" Max called after her, deflated. He told himself she was a human being, not some otherworldly goddess. He told himself he should just talk to her, but the thought made him feel the way the ferry ride to Catalina Island had on his ninth birthday: weak-kneed and queasy. How was it possible that he'd fallen for her so hard in just two weeks?

As Max shouldered his backpack and walked up the concrete steps, he cut past six of his classmates, all of them crowded together and gossiping about the old Sanderson house at the edge of town.

"I'm telling you, we should go there before the party," said a girl in an orange turtleneck. Over the turtleneck, she wore a slouchy blue sweater patterned with pumpkins.

"No way," whined her friend, who wore a red vest over a white sweater and looked more excited for Christmas than Halloween. She leaned against the front steps' metal handrail. "I'm not going anywhere near that house. It's creepy."

Max had to agree with the second girl. He'd seen the Sanderson house the previous weekend on a ride, and its rotting walls and sagging windows seemed to peer out of the woods as he cruised past. He'd also noticed the CLOSED INDEFINITELY signs tied along the wrought-iron fence that separated the Sanderson house—and much of Salem Wood—from the actual town of Salem.

A boy who wore a brown sweater over a white shirt threw an arm around the shoulders of the girl in the red vest. "I'll just have to hold you closer, Tess," he teased, grinning.

Tess beamed up at him. "My hero," she sighed, and then snorted. As her head settled on the boy's chest, their semicircle of friends laughing along with her, Max felt the seed of a plan begin to take root. . . .

Max wasn't sure why everyone filing into US History at the end of the day had grins on their faces. The classroom looked as it had for the past few weeks, with orange construction paper tacked to the pushpin boards that flanked the chalkboard at the front of the room. On one side was a silhouette of a frightened black cat, and on another a silhouette of a witch on her broom. Above the chalkboard, Miss Olin had replaced the framed portraits of her four favorite presidents with pen-and-ink drawings of four people involved in the Salem witch trials.

Miss Olin herself sat at her desk while the class filed in, scribbling notes to herself among an array of miniature pumpkins. There was a creepy little witch doll propped up at the front edge of her desk. It was dressed in a black-and-white Pilgrim's costume and a pointed hat with an orange ribbon for decoration—exactly like the one Miss Olin herself wore that day.

Max took his seat in the third row, beside the girl in the red vest and just a few desks away from Allison Watts. After the bell rang, Miss Olin explained—for his benefit, he supposed—that Salem tradition dictated that on All Hallows' Eve, each class's history teacher recounted the town's most popular Halloween story: one that had real witches and bubbling cauldrons and unbreakable spells. The way she said it made Max realize she was trying to express what a great honor this was for her, but he found himself concentrating on not rolling his eyes.

But when Miss Olin began to tell a story about the Sanderson sisters—who had lured a girl into the woods and killed her, then turned her brother into a cat—Max knew there was someone smiling down on him.

All he had to do was provoke Allison into an argument, which would give him an excuse to apologize and invite her to check out the Sanderson house. It wouldn't be hard. This may have been only his second Friday at Jacob Bailey High, but he knew Allison couldn't stand it when people fibbed their way through a class discussion. He'd learned that the hard way when he'd tried to impress her on Tuesday by swaggering through a devil's advocate position about states' rights—something he knew next to nothing about. He found that while Allison might be willing to help people with homework before class, she didn't find it charming if she thought you were making a mockery of something she cared about. She'd taken no prisoners, and he'd gone straight home to actually read the chapter about the Continental Congress.

But now he would use one of his new talents—specifically, being publicly humiliated by Allison Watts—to his advantage.

"And so," said Miss Olin, the very tip of her witch's hat bobbing as she spoke, "the Sanderson sisters were hanged by the Salem townsfolk. Now, there are those who say that on Halloween night a black cat still guards the old Sanderson house, warning off any who might make the witches come back to life!" With a

loud pop, a mess of streamers shot from her hand onto the nearest girl, making the whole class jump. Max had to admit it was a nice touch.

It was also his cue.

"Gimme a break," he sighed.

Miss Olin turned an arched eyebrow on him. "Aha," she said. "We seem to have a skeptic in our midst. Mr. Dennison, would you care to share your California, laid-back, tie-dyed point of view?"

The class howled with laughter and Max again had to restrain himself from rolling his eyes at his US History teacher. She wasn't the one whose feathers he needed to ruffle.

"Okay, granted that you guys in Salem are all into these black cats and witches and stuff—"

"*Stuff?*" gasped an affronted Miss Olin.

"Fine," Max pressed on. "But everyone knows that Halloween was invented by the candy companies."

The class groaned.

"It's a conspiracy," insisted Max.

"It just so happens," said Allison, like clockwork, "that Halloween is based on the ancient feast called All Hallows' Eve." Max and the rest of the class turned to watch her take him apart. She leaned forward and spoke directly to him while she did it.

Her expression was serious, and for a moment Max worried he'd really put his foot in it. "It's the one night of the year where the spirits of the dead can return to earth."

The class cheered and Allison smiled and accepted a high five from the pumpkin-sweatered girl who sat behind Max. At least she wasn't actually that upset, he reasoned. Having the whole class turn against him was a little embarrassing, but ultimately Max didn't care that they were celebrating his humiliation. He was already tearing a sheet of paper from his notebook and scribbling down his name. He'd pay Dani her weight in gummy pizzas to keep her away from *this* call.

He got up from his desk. "Well," he said, crossing the narrow aisle. "In case Jimi Hendrix shows up tonight, here's my number." He handed Allison the folded sheet of paper.

The class whooped.

Allison raised her eyebrows at him but didn't answer.

Max's heart slammed against his ribcage, a rubber ball trying to escape this risk-taking madman.

The bell rang and the class swirled out, Allison with them. Max scrambled to pack up his books and catch her before he lost his courage. Maybe if she gave him a chance, he'd actually make friends in Salem, and then Jack wouldn't have to lend Max his spare bunk after all.

Hundreds of students pressed through the halls of the high school and spilled out onto the street. In the anonymity of the crowd, a couple of students popped off black-and-orange streamers. A boy with a dancing skeleton knitted on his beanie shouted, "What do we want?"

"Ghosts!" shouted back the rest of the school.

"When do we want 'em?"

"Now!"

Max pushed his way through the celebrants, still baffled by their unselfconscious love of something meant for little kids.

He was grateful that Allison wore a bright red coat, because it helped him keep track of her in the outgoing tide of students.

He grabbed his bike and raced after her, slowing only because he was afraid of becoming a gross sweaty mess. His heart was beating hard enough for what he was about to do. He was going to speak with Allison, just the two of them, and he was going to invite her to visit the Sanderson house with him, and she was going to say yes, because if she didn't, he really would have to hitchhike back to LA, since the embarrassment of seeing her in class every day would be too much when all his friends were three thousand miles away. Max's parents and sister kept telling him to make the most of this move, and there he was, pedaling after his moon shot.

As he biked, he decided that he'd never seen so much Halloween decor in one place—not even in the holiday section of a department store. There were homemade ghosts and plastic zombies and giant googly eyes stuck in trees. People had even put up yellow and orange lights, and one man was testing the fog machine in his yard before the night's main event.

Max swung past a honking car and into Salem Common, the big park that sat in the middle of town. "Allison!" he barked before he could stop himself. He startled himself even, his foot slipping and causing him to skid to a halt.

She turned and eyed him for a second before saying, "Hi." She kept walking, but she slowed a little.

"Hi," he said, toeing his way after her. "Look—I'm sorry. I didn't mean to embarrass you in class."

"You didn't." She stopped then, and Max did, too.

He took a deep breath and told himself to play it cool.

"My name is Max Dennison," he said, extending a hand.

Allison softened. "Yeah, I know," she said, accepting his handshake.

Her palm was soft and warm against his, and he thought of the intricate vases he'd seen her carrying out of the arts wing—enough to stock a mansion, because, he suspected, she'd keep working at it until one came out perfect. He wondered whether asking about her ceramics class would make him seem thoughtful or creepy.

"You just moved here, huh?" she asked, saving him the embarrassment.

"Yeah, two weeks ago." He grabbed his handlebars so she wouldn't notice his shaking hands.

"Must be a big change for you."

"That's for sure."

She smiled. "You don't like it here?"

With two questions, Max felt like this conversation was really on a roll. He shrugged. "Oh, the leaves are great," he said, looking up at their fiery underbellies, "but . . . I dunno. Just all this Halloween stuff."

"You don't believe in it?"

"What do you mean, like the Sanderson sisters? No way."

"Not even on Halloween?"

His heart soared. He wasn't from Salem, but this was something he could work with: the universal teenage language of apathy. "*Especially* not on Halloween," he said.

Allison seemed to hesitate, and Max wondered whether he'd misread something. No one his age could actually believe in witches and flying broomsticks and newt-eye potions. Could they?

But Allison just smiled and offered him a folded piece of paper, more suave than he could ever hope to be. "Trick or treat," she said. The look she gave him made his bones melt.

She walked off then, pulling up her red hood against the October chill.

Max smiled to himself, and for a moment he wasn't even upset that he'd forgotten to ask her about visiting the Sanderson house. He'd spoken to Allison one-on-one, and she hadn't laughed at him or anything. Maybe this meant they could be friends. Maybe it even meant that one day, if he didn't mess things up, they could be something more than that.

Max unfolded the note and saw his own name and phone number, and his stomach sank. He turned over the paper, but there wasn't anything else written on any part of it.

He *had* misread her, though he wasn't sure how. And then he'd blown it.

Max sighed and looked down at the sidewalk. At least he still had his sweet new shoes. He decided to take the long way home to get some time to think.

He pedaled hard through Salem, avoiding anyone who might want to talk with him—an admittedly limited group since he was so new in town—and only slowed when he reached the edge of the graveyard marked by a wrought-iron gate topped with the words OLD BURIAL HILL.

He realized it was very broody to spend time in a cemetery, but it was also a peaceful place with rolling hills and craggy rocks that, on the northern rise, overlooked Salem and the harbor. Seeing the ocean had given him a comforting feeling his very first day in Salem. It reminded him of home and of the unending expanse of the Pacific. The idea that this place was even a little like LA made his heart ache, but it also made him feel like maybe he really could make the most of it here. Maybe his life didn't have to be so different after all.

The crest of the cemetery's hill was the kind of place he'd want to take Allison one day, after they'd gotten to know each other enough that she didn't think he was secretly an axe murderer. They could watch the ships come in and go out, cutting through deep blue water with rolling whitecaps, and wait for the lighthouse to come on as the sun started to go down. He could tell her about California and listen while she explained why she liked Salem, and maybe he'd find a way to like it, too.

Max rounded a section of tombstones, heading for the top of the hill.

Just then, a boy shouted, "Halt!"

Max stopped, confused, and turned to see Jay Taylor, the blond portion of the duo that terrorized Salem with poorly constructed bottle rockets and the occasional roll of toilet paper. Max groaned inwardly. Just then, Ernie popped up from behind a particularly large gravestone.

Max looked from Jay, with his straight shoulder-length hair and fingerless gloves, to Ernie, whose brown windbreaker was still too large for his thick torso, and he wondered how they'd befriended each other on the playground.

Jay tossed his blond hair. "Who are you?"

Max debated pedaling away, but the front of his bike was pointed uphill and it would take too long to swing it around. Besides, this day had to come sooner or later.

"Max," he said shortly. "I just moved here."

"From where?" Jay asked.

"Los Angeles."

Jay gave him a perplexed look and Max realized that this might be the first person he'd encountered who was too stupid to provide a "surf's up" joke. He counted his blessings.

"LA," he clarified.

"Oh!" said Jay happily. "Duuude!"

"Tubular," said Ernie.

That train was never late. Max took a steadying breath through his nose.

"I'm Jay," said Jay. "This is Ernie."

Ernie grabbed the elbow of Jay's black pleather jacket and pulled him into a crouch. "How many times I gotta tell you?" he grumbled. "My name ain't Ernie no more. It's Ice."

"This is Ice," Jay clarified, pointing.

Ernie spun around to show off the back of his head, where his nickname was shaved in block letters.

Max chuckled. He suddenly wasn't sure why he'd been worried about these two at all.

"So," said Jay, jumping down from the gravestone he'd been perched on. "Let's have a butt."

"No, thanks," said Max. "I don't smoke."

"They're very health-conscious in Los Angeles," mocked Ernie.

Jay broke into raucous laughter, and Ernie followed suit. They gave each other a double high five and a chest bump, and Max wondered how long he'd be stuck in this new-kid hazing ritual.

"You got any cash, Hollywood?" asked Jay, coming around to block Max's way. He leaned forward on Max's handlebars.

Max felt his pulse hiccup. "No," he said, trying to regain control of the bike.

"Gee," said Ernie, grabbing Max's biceps.

Max turned to him, and his heart was full-on pattering. He'd waited around too long, and even if these two were dumb, they were still bigger than him and seemed to have twitchy moral compasses.

"We don't get any smokes from you. We don't get any cash. What am I supposed to do with my afternoon?" said Jay.

Max inhaled slowly. "Maybe learn to breathe through your nose," he said.

Jay guffawed and quickly pretended to find the ground very interesting. "Whoa," he said, noticing Max's shoes. "Check out the new cross-trainers."

Max tried to pull away, but Ernie was even stronger than he looked.

"Cool," Ernie said to Jay, his grip on Max's arm tightening even further. "Let me try 'em on."

Max looked from one boy to the other, hoping they were joking. The Nikes had been the only good thing about his move to Salem.

Ernie gave him a look that said *I'm waiting*, and before Max knew it, he was biking away from them shoeless, the treads of his pedals sharp and uncomfortable even through his socks.

At least they hadn't thought to take his bike, he told himself. He was angry at himself for not getting away before Jay and Ernie cornered him. He was mad at his dad for accepting the transfer to a new management position in Salem. And he was mad at Dani for making the move look so easy when it was clearly so painfully lame.

At the top of Old Burial Hill, the cemetery chapel chimed four o'clock. Max sighed and continued biking down the hill, back toward town. Both of his parents would be home by now, as would Dani.

He'd lost his Nikes, his shot with Allison, and his chance at privacy—and it wasn't even dinnertime.

Once home, Max went straight up to his room and flopped onto the bed.

He hated the sailboat wallpaper of his room almost as much

as he did the pale purple paint that trimmed the steps leading to the small loft overhead.

He'd tried to make it look more like his last room, carefully placing his drum set to take up as much space as possible. He'd even tacked up the tie-dyed blanket Jack sent him after Max told him about the California hippie jokes.

None of his attempts, though, had worked. This old nursery didn't look anything like his room, and staring at it just made him feel more alone. So he glared at the white popcorn ceiling and listened to the quiet bubbling of the fish tank beside his bed.

The bike ride home hadn't calmed his anger—if anything, the pedals cutting into his feet had stoked it. Why couldn't his parents have waited two more years before moving? Then he'd have graduated and gone to college and they could have moved Dani anywhere they liked. Besides, who transferred their kids to a new school in the middle of *October*?

Max squeezed his eyes shut and sighed. October made him think about Halloween, which made him think about Allison and her note. He'd really blown it, and he still didn't get how.

Did Allison like Halloween because she liked to dress up, or because of this weird, witchy town, or because she actually believed in spells that could transform people into immortal cats? Max wasn't sure which option he preferred. He rolled over. As if it mattered. As if he'd have a chance with her either way.

"Allison," he sighed, remembering her hand in his when he'd introduced himself—his smoothest move of the day. "You're so soft," he continued. "I just want to—"

His closet burst open. Max sat up with a racing pulse.

"Boo!" Dani cackled, applauding herself for such a good prank. She was still in her costume, and her patterned skirt swished as she danced. "I scared you! I scared you!"

Max blushed.

Dani clambered over him and tossed herself onto his bed. She thrashed about, crooning, "I'm Allison! Kiss me, I'm Allison!"—which only made Max blush harder.

He stood up. "Mom and Dad told you to stay out of my room!"

"Don't be such a crab," Dani said, rolling her eyes. She stood up on his mattress to make herself taller, then began to jump, the yellow-and-orange fringe of her jacket swinging wildly. The mattress springs protested each time she landed. "Guess what?" she asked. Then, before he could answer: "You're going to take me trick-or-treating."

She couldn't be serious. "Not this year, Dani."

Dani twirled and leaped off the bed. "Mom said you have to."

"Well," said Max, "she can take you."

"She and Dad are going to the Pumpkin Ball downtown," she protested, tugging on his sleeve.

"You're eight," he said, jerking away from her. "Go by yourself." He crossed the room, sat down at his drum set, and tapped out a beat on the snare.

"No way," said Dani. "This is my first time! I'll get lost. Besides, it's a full moon outside. The weirdos are out."

Max ignored her, throwing in the hi-hat. If Jack had been there, he would've plugged in his guitar and they'd have been halfway through "London Calling" by now.

Dani threw her arms around his neck. "Come on, Max," she said.

He sighed and let his sticks settle across one knee.

"Can't you forget about being a cool teenager for one night?" she begged. "Please come out. We used to have so much fun together trick-or-treating. Remember? It'll be like old times."

He jerked away. "The old days are dead," he said, restarting the beat. He knew he'd end up taking her, but he wished to god she'd just give him five minutes alone. He needed to think. He needed to listen to Green Day. He needed to *not* walk around with his kid sister dressed as Winona the Whimsical Witch.

"It doesn't matter *what* you say," Dani declared. "You're taking me."

Max tossed down his sticks. "Wanna bet?" He crossed the room again, this time climbing into the small loft that was the best part of his new room. The best part of Massachusetts, as far as he was concerned, especially now that Allison thought he was an idiot and his sneakers were getting stretched out by Ernie's clubfeet. He crossed his arms and leaned against the wall.

Dani's eyes narrowed and she did the thing that always turned arguments in her favor.

She screamed for their mother.

Dani and Max had only been trick-or-treating for ten minutes, but Max was already angling to go home.

Before leaving the house, Dani had begged him to put on a costume, and he'd relented by pulling on sunglasses, a baseball cap, and an oversize suede jacket that belonged to their dad. He pulled the brim low as they walked, and the grimace on his face said that there was no universe in which this night would turn out to be fun for him.

"Lighten up, Max," Dani said, leading him to the next house. He plopped onto the porch step to wait as she sidled up to the door after a pink princess and a pirate.

"What a festive little witch you are," said the woman who answered the door.

Max rolled his eyes.

When Dani came back, pleased with both her haul and the compliment, she handed Max the extra candy bar she'd taken for him.

"Can we go home now?" he asked, dropping the chocolate into his bag.

"No."

As they headed back down the walk toward the street, Max groaned. "Dani—" he started, but it was too late. Jay and Ernie had rolled up and were holding court with their goons. Jay was in a pumpkin-smashing contest with a beanie-wearing sophomore, and Ernie was perched on the brick-and-concrete wall of the steps that Max and Dani had to take to return to the street.

Max pivoted, deciding to cut across the lawn and walk down the driveway of the neighboring house. Dani did not get the memo.

"Ding, ding, ding, ding," Ernie trilled.

At that, Jay hurried over to Dani. "Stop and pay the toll, kid."

"Ten chocolate bars, no licorice," added Ernie.

"Dump out your sack."

Dani wrinkled her brow, unimpressed. "Drop *dead*, moron."

Around them, the boys in denim jackets and ill-advised hats let out a chorus of shocked, delighted whoops and whistles.

"Yo, twerp," Ernie quickly cut in, "how'd you like to be hung off that telephone pole?"

"I'd like to see you try," said Dani. "It just so happens I've got my big brother with me." She looked over her shoulder at Max, who was staying in the background—dreaming of dodging the boys by heading down the block but not willing to abandon his sister. "Max!" Dani said.

"Hollywood!" Ernie called in recognition.

Max stuffed his hands into his pockets and looked away.

This time, the swell of sound bubbled with laughter. "Awkward," intoned a guy with the world's smallest ear gauges.

"So," said Jay, swaggering over to Max, "you're doing a little trick-or-treating." He mimicked the action with Ernie, which gained a cheap laugh from their friends.

"I'm just taking my little sister around," Max said, stepping into Jay's personal space.

Jay hummed. "That's nice," he said. He slapped down the brim of Max's ball cap. "Wow! I love the costume." He leaned in close. "But what are you supposed to be? A New Kid on the Block?" He grabbed Max's elbow to keep himself from falling over as he cracked up at his own joke.

"For your information," Dani announced, "he's a *little leaguer.*"

The boys laughed hard at that, with Ernie pretending to strike a pitch from Jay with a tiny invisible bat.

Max shouldered past them.

"Wait a minute," said Ernie, grabbing Max's shoulder. "Everybody pays the toll."

"Stuff it, zit face," said Dani.

Ernie dropped Max's jacket to turn on her. "Why, you little—"

"Hey!" Max interrupted, putting himself between Dani and the bullies. "Ice, here," he said, and pressed his own paper bag of candy into Ernie's thick chest. "Pig out." He took his sister by the arm. "Come on, Dani. Let's go."

As he stalked down the block, Dani skipping to keep up with him, he heard Ernie send a last volley across the road: "And, Hollywood, the shoes fit great!"

Max let go of Dani's arm and shoved his hands into his coat pockets, his face burning.

He didn't say anything as they made their way down the block. He could tell Dani was disappointed in him, which only made him more annoyed with her. It was great that she thought he could take ten other guys in a fight—but seriously? Now Jay and Ernie would never forget his face. And now that he'd given them both his shoes and his candy without fighting back, they'd never leave him alone.

He followed Dani up the front steps to another house.

"Should've punched him," Dani finally grumbled. She didn't look at Max.

Her flip suggestion made Max's irritation flare. "He would've killed me!"

"At least you would've died like a man," she replied.

"Hey!" Max imagined that Allison would have kept her cool and turned Dani's gendered stereotyping into a teaching moment, as she'd done when their geometry teacher made a joke about girls being bad at math, but right now he was just afraid that his little sister might be right. "You just humiliated me in front of half the guys at school," he told her hotly. "So collect your candy and get out of my life."

Dani's eyes filled with tears. She brushed past him on her way back down the steps. "I wanna go home. Now."

Max sighed as she dashed through the yard and down the sidewalk. He hadn't really meant that—and he certainly shouldn't have said it out loud. It wasn't Dani's fault that Jay and Ernie and their gang were so awful.

There was a display of haystacks and seasonal decor in front of another house, and she tackled one of the pumpkins as if it were one of the fluffy pillows on her bed.

"Dani," Max said, walking over, "I'm sorry." He sat down heavily on the hay next to his shaking, sobbing sister. "It's just that I hate this place," he said, snatching off his ball cap. "I miss all my friends. I wanna go home."

"*This* is your home now," Dani said over her shoulder, "so get used to it." She sniffled and wiped snot from her nose.

Max sighed. If only it were that easy. Dani had always been better at rolling with the punches. But he also knew that just because she was, that didn't mean he should take out his own dislike of change on her. He leaned over. "Yeah," he admitted. Then he asked gently, "Gimme one more chance?"

"Why should I?"

"'Cause I'm your brother."

She turned to look at him, and Max gave her an exaggerated pout. She giggled, and the sound of her laugh made him smile, too.

Max looked up past the glare of the streetlights.

"Whoa," he said, "check that out."

"What?" asked Dani seriously.

The two of them stood up.

"Something just flew across the moon," Max said.

Dani wandered closer to the street, craning her neck.

Max glanced down at her, smirked, and grabbed her around the waist, shouting.

She squealed, breaking into another wave of giggles.

"Fooled ya," Max said, dusting hay off her jacket.

Dani relaxed for a moment against her big brother, and for a second it felt like they were back home in Southern California, happy. "Let's go, jerk face," she said, tugging on his sleeve.

They turned down the walk to the closest house and gasped in unison.

CHAPTER 2

**HECK OUT** this house." Max ogled the building, which was at least two stories tall, though light glowed warm through a series of windows in the roof, as well, suggesting a finished attic.

The house itself was made of white clapboard, with dark shutters framing each window. Candlelit jack-o'-lanterns, poised behind thick windowpanes and lining the red-brick walk, peered at them. The sounds of a party spilled down the front steps and through the iron gate to where Max and Dani stood, looking like dumbstruck street urchins.

Max felt a pang of envy, but Dani interrupted before he could truly wallow.

"Rich people," she said matter-of-factly, shrugging. "They'll probably make us drink cider and bob for apples."

Max looked down at her, wondering how a girl her age could be so good at keeping things in perspective. Despite her prediction, she dashed up the steps and pushed open the door. Max joined her, taking in the party.

The entry hall was bigger than his and Dani's new bedrooms combined, with a staircase sweeping up one side. In the adjoining room, adults his parents' age milled around sipping wine. They were all dressed in frilly, expensive-looking clothes that reminded Max of Marie Antoinette. In a far corner, a pianist and string quartet played discreetly.

"Is this for real?" Max breathed.

"Jackpot!" Dani had honed in on the cauldron of candy on a table in the middle of the entryway. They dashed over to it together, and Max plunged both hands in, feeling a giddiness he hadn't experienced since he was close to Dani's age. The cauldron was almost overflowing with full-size 100 Grand and Oh Henry! bars, plus Gobstoppers, Butterfinger BB's, and chocolate lollipops shaped like witches and Frankenstein's monster. Dani picked up a witch wrapped in cellophane and ran a finger over the warty nose reverentially, as if she could get a sugar high just from touching it.

"Max Dennison." The girl's voice sounded like she'd caught

a toddler with his hand in the cookie jar—or in this case, the candy cauldron.

Max looked up to find Allison on the second-floor landing, leaning over the wooden handrail. Like the older women downstairs, she wore a long silk dress with lots of trim and complicated buttons. The cream sleeves of the dress ended at her elbows and turned into a waterfall of white lace. She wore an expensive-looking necklace, too, made of fat white pearls and one of those medallions with a Victorian woman's profile carved into it. The dress didn't seem like Allison's style, but the smile on her

face—big and broad and a bit sly—was all her, and it made Max's heart do a complicated flip.

"Allison," he said, stepping away from the candy cauldron.

"Oh," Dani said conspiratorially. Her eyes darted from her brother to the girl at the top of the staircase. "*Allison.*"

Max shot her a death look.

Allison grabbed her flouncy skirts to prevent herself from tripping down the steps. "I thought you weren't into Halloween," she said, making her way toward them.

"I'm not," said Max. "I'm just taking my sister, Dani, around."

"That's nice," said Allison, smiling.

Max's stomach turned into a warm, melty mess. He'd never made Allison smile like that before—not like she was being polite but like she was actually impressed. He grinned back and put an arm around Dani's shoulders. "I always do it," he said proudly.

"My parents made him," said Dani smartly.

Max nudged her.

Allison's smile grew bigger as she watched the two siblings tease each other. "Do you guys want some cider?"

"Sure," said Max before Dani could protest. He shot her a warning look when Allison's back was turned as she headed into the adjoining room, but Dani only smirked at him.

Allison filled two orange paper cups with warm cider and returned to them.

"Thanks," said Max, taking the cup she offered him. "How's the party?"

"Boring," said Allison. "It's just a bunch of my parents' friends. They do this every year." She walked back over to the cauldron and gestured. "And I get candy duty. By the way, Dani, I love your costume."

"Thank you," said Dani. "I really like yours, too. Of course, I couldn't wear anything like that, because I don't have"—she paused, turning innocently to her brother—"what do you call them, Max? Yabos?"

Max choked on his cider. The sting of cinnamon and powdered cloves went up his nose.

"Max likes your yabos," Dani said. "In fact, he loves them."

Max looked apologetically at Allison, trying to convey both abject horror and *kids will be kids*, but probably just managing to look like a stalker.

Allison laughed and picked out a few more pieces of candy for Dani.

Max, meanwhile, wondered how he could possibly redeem himself, or at least explain himself. He also wondered whether his parents would mind if Dani mysteriously went missing and ended up living with their aunt in Seattle.

"I'm really into witches," said Allison, admiring Dani's costume.

Max was too relieved by the change in topic to be annoyed that they were again talking about witches as if they were baseball cards or Bon Jovi.

"Really? Me too." Dani unwrapped her chocolate witch and nibbled on the tip of her hat. "We just learned about those sisters in school."

"You mean the Sanderson sisters?" A look of real excitement came over Allison's face, the way it did when Miss Olin started talking about the Bill of Rights in US History. "I know all about them," she went on. "My mom used to run the museum."

Dani grinned, equally excited. "There's a museum about them?"

"Yeah, but they shut it down because"—Allison leaned in and lowered her voice to a whisper—"a lot of *spooky things* happened there."

Max felt like his plan had boomeranged and fallen in his lap, and he wasn't about to let it slip away again. "Why don't we go to the old Sanderson house?" he asked. He hoped he sounded fearless and cool, especially since his attempts to impress her up till then had come off more like schoolyard teasing.

Allison turned to him, startled.

Dani shook her head, looking frightened, which confused Max because she'd seemed so excited just ten seconds before.

"Well, come on," he said to Allison. "Make a believer out of me."

Allison met his eyes, and he couldn't stop himself from smiling.

He was surprised when she smiled back. "Okay," she said, smoothing her skirts. "Let me get changed. They'll never miss me."

When Allison was on her way up the stairs, Dani turned on Max. "We're not going up there," she insisted. "My friends at school told me all about that place. It's weird."

"Dani." He touched her wrist, but his eyes didn't leave Allison. "This is the girl of my dreams."

"So take her to the movies like a normal person," Dani insisted.

"Dani!" Once Allison had rounded a corner at the top of the stairs, Max sighed and sank down onto one knee, facing his sister. "Look, just do this one thing for me, and I'll do anything you say. Please?" he pleaded.

Dani looked thoughtful.

Max didn't know why Allison was giving him the time of day now, after blowing him off only a few hours before, but he suspected it had something to do with Dani. He wasn't going to let this second chance—or his little sister—get away from him.

"Please?" he begged, clasping his hands. "Please?"

Dani patted his shoulder to quiet him. "Okay. Next year we go trick-or-treating as Wendy and Peter Pan"—she leaned in close, her nose almost touching his—"*with* tights, or it's no deal."

Max looked longingly at the empty staircase.

Dani shrugged and spun away.

"Okay, okay," he said, grabbing her around the middle before she got too far. Like it or not, Allison seemed more relaxed when Dani was around. And like it or not, he felt more relaxed, too. Was that weird? He didn't have time to psychoanalyze. "Deal," he said. "Deal."

Dani beamed and slapped his back.

CHAPTER 3

LLISON LED the way, though Max knew exactly where they were going, too. She cut through the grave-yard, which made Max nervous they might come across Jay and Ernie again. The last thing he needed was to be forced into a fight to defend Allison's honor—or his own.

The graveyard was eerie at night. It seemed less like a place to watch Salem Harbor and more like a place to perform weird occult rituals. The tombstones resembled crooked teeth, and the linden trees towered like gaunt, broken-boned skeletons watching them in the dark.

Dani clutched Max's forearm the whole time, and though her

nails were clipped too short to dig into Max's skin, he could feel the press of her fingertips through his jacket. It almost made him feel bad about the whole thing, but he reasoned that she'd go to school the next week with the best story in her class. Really, he was doing her a favor.

They exited the graveyard, and Allison led them all the way down the street to the corner with the stop sign. She took Dani's right hand in hers, and Dani still clung tight to Max's wrist, and a fluttering feeling stirred in his belly. It was almost like he was holding Allison's hand. He'd never thought about whether or not she'd get along with Dani, but he liked that she did and he liked that she tried, and he liked that she took them to the crosswalk to teach Dani good road etiquette.

A stone wall bordered the sidewalk. It was made of big river-tumbled rocks stuck together with crumbling mortar and stitched even more securely with creeping ivy.

"Legend has it that the bones of one hundred children are buried within these walls," said Allison, running her fingers along the time-polished stones.

"Oh, great."

Allison let go of Dani's hand as they approached a wrought-iron gate. "You ready?" she asked, looking from Dani to Max.

Max nodded, pressing Dani against his hip in case she tried to book it.

"Tights," she muttered, meeting his eyes.

He nodded.

Allison looked at them both like they were on something, but she pulled an old key out of her sweater and unlocked the gate.

The three of them stepped through it, and something small and dark shot across the path in front of them.

Dani jumped and, short or not, this time Max felt the bite of her nails.

"What was that?" she hissed.

Max dragged her forward, taking her torso with him as if her feet were rooted to the ground. "It's just a cat," he said, then knelt and pointed at a fallen tree to show her. Two yellow-green eyes caught the light of a distant streetlamp.

"It's not just a cat," said Allison. "It's *the* cat. The one that warns you not to go in. It's been here as long as I can remember."

"How long do cats live?" Dani whispered urgently.

Max felt around in the fallen leaves and picked up a pebble. He chucked it toward the glowing eyes, prompting a yowl.

The cat disappeared.

Dani and Allison both looked at Max, disgusted.

"I didn't think I'd hit it," he said.

Dani sighed and looked at Allison. "Max failed out of baseball camp," she said, sounding resigned. They started up the buckling path.

"I did not *fail*," said Max.

"Fine. Max came home crying from baseball camp."

"That was a long time ago. How do you even remember?"

"My blackmail book," said Dani.

The walkway petered out long before they reached the house, and the three of them were forced to tromp through a thick carpet of dead leaves. Max stepped down on a spindly fallen tree, applying all his weight to make it easier for the girls to pass. Allison steadied herself on his shoulder as she did, which made Max swallow hard.

The house ahead of them was smaller than Max expected, but somehow it seemed to loom above them, as if its spirit were far bigger than the collapsing wooden porch and broken eaves. Max eyed it, feeling uncertain. He knew he was the one who'd suggested this field trip, but he was beginning to think the place would cave in on them—or at least give them all tetanus.

The low wooden steps creaked as Max climbed them.

"I don't think we should go in," said Dani.

Max gave her a look and she rolled her eyes.

"Sure," she said. "Whatever."

Allison produced a second key and unlocked the door. The sound of the deadbolt disengaging was loud and final.

Max looked back at Dani, who was chewing her bottom lip as if debating whether to walk home by herself. Finally, she sighed and tromped up the stairs. She muttered something about "stupid crushes" as she flipped a switch on her plastic candy bucket and lifted the jack-o'-lantern's glowing face. She led the way into the house, closely followed by Max and Allison.

"I can't see a thing," Dani said.

"There's a light switch around here somewhere," said Allison.

Max took Dani's makeshift flashlight and peered around.

When Max had biked past the previous weekend, he'd thought the house seemed creepy in an old dilapidated way, but now he realized that it was sinister in a far different manner. The air inside was both stale and a little too still—the way a house feels when everyone is playing hide-and-seek. Still, yet tingling with nerves. Still, yet anxiously watching.

A ticket counter at the front of the room displayed dusty tchotchkes, including postcards of Salem, and stuffed bears with patterned capes and tiny brooms, and—

"Found a lighter," Max said, plucking a Zippo from the display case. The silver lighter was engraved with a witch silhouetted against a full moon.

He struck it and hurried over to the wall to help Allison locate the light switch. It was an industrial thing that had only been installed in the past decade or so, but when they flipped the switch it didn't work.

"Try the breaker box," said Allison, pointing. Max opened the metal panel and turned every breaker off and then on again. This time, the lights throughout the room popped to life.

The main part of the house was one big room with wood floors and wood walls and a high wood ceiling. There was a loft on one side of the house, which reminded Max of the small loft in his own room. A broom was mounted near the loft, with a helpful plaque identifying it as a witch's broom, in case visitors weren't sure about the house's shtick.

There were other signs of a modern influence, too. In addition to the electric lights, narrow piping ran around the perimeter of the ceiling, each branch ending with a spigot: sprinklers in case the old tinderbox went up in flames, Max realized.

Also, the layout of the room was that of a museum, not everyday living. The furniture had been moved back from the middle of the room to make way for a series of displays that had become overrun with spiderwebs in the absence of regular cleaning. On one wall was a huge curio cabinet loaded with bottles and jars. Nearby, a set of cast-iron pots and pans hung from hooks in the ceiling. Everything had a small plaque with a glaringly obvious explanation.

"Here's the original cauldron," Allison said, pointing to the squat iron pot hung above an empty circle of stones. "Upstairs is where they slept," she said, gesturing to the loft. She came around to a display case featuring a large leather-bound book. It was the biggest book Max had ever seen, as long as his forearm and thicker than the width of his hand. The cover was held together with wide, angry-looking stitches, and swirls of tarnished silver helped reinforce the corners and the spine. Along the right edge of the cover was a strange pucker of leather—almost like the closed eye of a rhinoceros, or of a person who spent far too much time in a tanning booth. A loop of silver surrounded that, too, the far edge of the metal turning into a latch that would have kept the book shut if there had been a padlock.

Allison leaned down to read the information card. "'It was given to her by the Devil himself. The book is bound in human skin and contains the recipes for her most powerful and evil spells.'"

She snuck a glance at Max's sister.

"I get the picture," Dani said.

Allison laughed. "According to town records, this went missing after the Sanderson sisters were hanged. They found it in another woman's house just a few days later. I guess she wanted to try it out for herself."

Dani shuddered. "How many witches does Salem have, anyway?"

"None anymore," Allison said, squeezing Dani's shoulder. "Present company excluded," she added, and tugged on the tip of Dani's hat. The little girl smiled.

"What's that?" Max asked. He crossed to the far corner of the room, where an ancient-looking cast-iron stand supported a tall cream-colored candle. Its surface was decorated with complicated etchings of trees and fire and, at the base, small humans running in fear. But they had nowhere to run since they always ran into one another.

"Oh." Allison pitched her voice low. "It's the Black Flame Candle."

Max looked at the nearby plaque. " 'Black Flame Candle. Made from the fat of a hanged man. Legend says that on a full moon, it will raise the spirits of the dead if lit by a virgin on Halloween night.' "

He looked around the quiet old museum. There was no one there but them, and this seemed like the perfect way to make their night more memorable. It would give Dani something else to tell her friends—and Allison, too. He liked the idea of Allison telling her friends about him, even if it was about him doing something silly.

"So let's light this sucker and meet the old broads," he said, pulling the lighter out of his pocket.

Dani, looking aghast, shook her head vehemently.

"Wanna do the honors?" Max asked Allison.

She was smiling but looked unimpressed. "No, thanks," she said, rolling her eyes.

It was the eye roll that threw him. Did that mean she *wasn't* a virgin? Did he care?

Out of nowhere, a screeching cat leaped onto the back of his neck. Its claws were sharp needles, and there were so damn many of them. Max fell to his knees, shouting. He wrestled it off and dropped hard onto his shoulder. The startled creature slunk under an old chest of drawers. "Stupid cat!"

"Okay, Max," said Dani. "You've had your fun. It's time to go. Come on, Allison." She took Allison by the hand, and the two of them headed for the door.

"Max, she's right," said Allison. "Let's go."

But Max had finally caught his breath. "Oh, come on," he said, not ready to head home just yet. He liked Allison, sure, but she was also the only person who'd given him the time of day in Salem, and he couldn't make it another two years there if he didn't have friends. "It's just a bunch of hocus-pocus."

That made Dani put on her mom voice: "Max, I'm not kidding this time," she said. "It's time to go."

Max shook his head at what a little kid Dani was being. Sometimes she acted so mature that he forgot, until moments like these, that she was only eight.

He opened the Zippo and held it to the candle's dusty wick.

"Max, no!" shouted Dani. The candle caught instantly, and Max grinned. But then he saw what a strange flame it was: it flickered yellow and orange around the edges but had a cool black heart.

Max's expression changed to one of concern. "Uh-oh."

CHAPTER 4

NE BY ONE, the light bulbs around the room burst in flashes of brilliant white. Each time, Dani squealed, her hands covering her eyes. Allison let out a quiet, frightened sound as the last bulb shattered and left them in the dark.

A breeze picked up, tumbling Dani's hat from her head. She uncovered her eyes and looked up, amazed. The heavy ironwork chandelier creaked loudly on its chain. Allison pulled Dani closer to her, and Max began to cross the room toward the two girls. A brilliant green light shot through the gaps in the floorboards, and the wood began to tremble and jump, threatening to rip away from the nails keeping it in place. Allison and Dani screamed, jumping toward the nearest wall. Max tried to steady himself by

grabbing on to some nearby furniture, but it felt like the whole house was shaking—and like the floor could very well decide to open up and drop them all into some unknown world.

Max was deciding whether to attempt a running leap at the door when the house stilled and went dark again. The three stood quiet for a moment, as if they weren't sure whether it would start all over again.

"What happened?" Max finally asked, breathless.

Dani picked up her witch's hat and shoved it back onto her head. "A virgin lit the candle," she said.

There was a sharp *pop*, and one by one the lights in the chandelier relit—this time with real flames. Around the room, candles came alive with a soft *whoosh*. Beneath the huge cauldron, an equally large fire roared to life, and the kitchen hearth fizzed as if someone had thrown in a handful of lit sparklers. The sparks quickly caught the display tinder and burst into a warm fire.

The air cracked open with a delighted cackle, and Allison and Dani dove away from the front door just as it blew open, its knob slamming into the wall.

Max had hidden, as well, ducking under a heavy dining table near the spell book's case. When he lowered himself to the ground and looked up at the door, his eyes grew wide.

Three women were silhouetted in milky moonlight and framed by the open door: the first with long blond hair and a

narrow waist, the second with two wild swoops of hair near the crown of her head, and the third with dark wiry curls twisted into the shape of a crooked cornucopia.

The woman in the middle marched into the house. She wore a floor-length emerald dress with a high collar and a creeping black pattern that seemed determined to smother the green. A gold clasp cinched the dress at her waist, and her underskirts were a brilliant blue. As she came into the light, the unnatural red of her hair became obvious. "We're home!" she declared.

Max felt dizzy. *This can't be happening,* he thought. *They can't be real.* He glanced in Allison's direction, but she was out of his line of sight. Was it a prank? A weird Salem-centric way of getting back at him after he made fun of Halloween? But he recalled the way the Black Flame Candle burned.

Beside the woman in green, the other two women clasped hands and began to dance and jump about, giggling. One—the blond one—wore a low-cut rosy dress with filmy sleeves that gathered at her wrists. The other wore layers and layers: an orange dress beneath a red vest and a matching wool cape. Her tartan skirts were intersecting lines of black and gray and, depending on the light, a dozen other colors.

"Oh, sweet revenge," said the redheaded witch. "You see, sisters? My curse worked perfectly."

"That's because thou art perfect, Winnie," said the brunette, touching her elder sister's shoulder. *She means Winifred*, thought Max, remembering Miss Olin's story. *Winifred Sanderson.*

The three witches laughed, and Winifred hurried across the room, her brunet sister trailing her.

The blond witch waited until they'd gone, then popped up onto her toes and reached into the rafters over the door. She was tall and thin, and her hair flowed in gentle waves down her back and over the creamy skin of her chest. She grinned as she found the thing she'd been feeling around for. She pulled down what appeared to be a length of twine.

"My lucky rat tail!" she crowed. "Just where I left it."

"But who lit the Black Flame Candle, hmmm?" Winifred asked, crossing toward the strange flame. She paused, fingers on her lips, then noticed the case with the huge spell book. She gave a delighted gasp and hurried over to it, tapping her long nails on the glass.

"Come on, sleepy head!" she cooed. "We have work to do. I missed you—did you miss me, too?"

The brunet sister sidled up behind her. "Winnie," she whispered.

"Yes, Mary?"

"I smell children."

"Sic 'em!"

The three witches slipped into line, with Mary leading. She sniffed the air eagerly.

"It's a little girl," she declared.

Behind her, the blond Sanderson nibbled the tip of her rat tail. Max knew that they were headed right for Dani, but he didn't know what to do. He spotted her crouched behind the old ticket-taking counter, chewing her bottom lip. He gauged the distance between himself and Mary, wondering how long he could keep the sisters occupied if he leaped out of hiding.

"Seven," Mary said, sniffing again. "Maybe eight. And a half."

"Let's play with her!" trilled the blonde.

"You'll frighten her, Sarah," said Winifred.

Sarah began to sing softly. "*Come out, little children; I'll take thee away—*"

Dani raised her eyes to the ceiling, pleading with some higher power to help her.

Winifred closed a hand over Sarah's mouth. "Come out, dear," she said. "We will not harm thee."

"We love children!" Mary agreed, slamming a hand on the counter.

Winifred gave her an ugly look, but it was quickly wiped away when Dani popped up in front of them.

"I thought thou'd never come, sisters," she said, adopting the worst British accent Max had ever heard.

"Greetings, little one," Winifred said warmly.

"'Twas I who brought you back."

"Imagine," said Winifred. "Such a pretty little"—she swallowed thickly—"child."

Sarah giggled.

"And she's so well fed, isn't she?" said Mary, going around the counter. "Plump!" she exclaimed, poking Dani in the ribs. Dani shrieked. "Plump!" Another jab, another squeal. "Plump! Shish ke-baby!"

Winifred rescued Dani just as Max was about to barrel across the room. "Tell me, dumpling," she said, placing Dani's hand on her arm as she led her deeper into the house, "what is the year?"

"Nineteen ninety-three."

Winifred pushed Dani into an ancient straight-backed dining chair.

"Sisters," she said eagerly, "we have been gone three hundred years."

"Well, Winnie, how time flies, huh?" said Mary. "When you're dead?"

The sisters all laughed, and Dani laughed, too, clearly hoping to please them. She kept going after they had finished, until her eyes landed on Mary's hungry face. Then her laughter died into a nervous chuckle. "It's been great fun," she said, getting up. "But I guess I'd better be going."

"Oh," Winifred said, pressing her back into the chair, "stay for supper."

"But I'm—I'm not hungry," said Dani.

"But we are," said Mary with a dangerous smile.

This time, when Dani tried to get up, Mary and Sarah each caught her by an arm and lifted her, kicking and screaming, toward the cauldron at the heart of the room.

"Hey!" shouted Max, springing out of his hiding place. "Let go of my little sister."

"Roast him, Winnie," Mary growled.

"No," Sarah breathed, touching Winifred's arm eagerly. "Let me—let me play with him."

Winifred heeded Mary rather than Sarah and shot a bolt of

bright, branching lightning at Max's chest. He lost consciousness briefly as he hit the ground but woke to a pain snaking through his whole body. He groaned.

"Max!" screamed Dani.

Winifred threw her magic at him again, dragging him across the floor and pinning him to the wall.

"I haven't lost my touch, sisters," she said, cackling. "See?" She flung him about to face her.

Max gasped at the feeling of knives in his bloodstream. The pain was sharp and sudden and made him think that his heart would give out. He tried to cover his chest, but his hands were pressed against the wall by an invisible force.

Sarah nestled into his neck. She smelled like wet earth and orange pomanders and honey.

"Hello," Winifred said to him. "Good-bye." This time her green lightning bolts lifted him from the ground. His body skimmed the wall, moving slowly to the ceiling. He couldn't see straight—could hardly keep enough wits about him to continue to breathe. He whimpered, but the sound was drowned out by the electric crackle and hum.

Mary held Dani tightly as the little girl shrieked her brother's name over and over again.

"Mary," Allison said, and as soon as the witch turned, she struck her over the head with the broom she'd retrieved from the wall display. As the brunet witch stumbled around, Allison grabbed a frying pan from the rack and slammed it over her head, making her hair even more crooked.

"You leave my brother alone!" Dani shouted at Winifred, then struck her with her bag of candy. She lashed out at Sarah, as well, for good measure.

Max crumpled to the ground, weak and exhausted.

When Dani crouched down to tend to him, the black cat reappeared and leaped onto Winifred's neck. It flexed its claws into the softest parts.

"Get him!" Winifred shrieked, spinning about. "Get this animal—get this beast off of me."

"Max, let's go," Dani said, pulling at his jacket. He forced himself up and stumbled after her toward the door, where Allison waited for them. He was about to join them when he realized they couldn't just leave the Sanderson sisters inside. They'd find their way to town eventually, and he didn't want that horrible lightning magic let loose on anyone else. The witches still struggled to get the cat off of Winifred, who spun wildly about.

"Get out!" he shouted at the two girls. "Go, go, go!"

The witches finally flung the cat off of Winifred.

Max stopped short before reaching the door. *How do you kill a witch?* he thought. In *The Wizard of Oz*, Dorothy did it with a bucket of water—but he didn't have a bucket.

Then he remembered the sprinklers.

When he was sure the girls were gone, he hoisted himself into the sleeping loft and rose on unsteady feet. "Hey!" he called, drawing the witches' attention up. "You have messed with the great and powerful Max and now must suffer the consequences. I summon the Burning Rain of Death."

The sisters tried to puzzle out what he meant, talking over one another.

"Burning what?" asked Sarah.

"Burning Rain of Death," repeated Winifred.

"What does he mean by—"

"Rain, did he say?" asked Mary.

"I don't know. Burning—"

Max drew out the lighter again and snapped it. When the flame popped up, the Sanderson sisters gasped.

"He makes fire in his hand," muttered Winifred, impressed.

Max lifted the lighter toward a spigot on the sprinkler system and waited until they all began spouting water throughout the house.

The Sanderson sisters screamed, rushing away to try to escape the falling water.

Max leaped down from the loft but slipped in a puddle, falling hard on his back.

The cat jumped onto his chest. "Nice job, Max."

Max gasped, recoiling. "You can talk."

"Yeah, no kidding," said the cat. "Now get the spell book."

Max couldn't move but wasn't sure whether that was from shock or a broken spine.

The cat batted a paw at Max's face. "Come on," he ordered, "move it!"

With that, Max shoved himself to his feet and grabbed one of the posts that held an information card for the witches' cauldron. He used it to shatter the glass to the spell book's case and pulled it out, ignoring the shards of glass that dug into his skin.

The witches were too afraid of the water to chase him, instead cowering in an alcove near the kitchen.

"My book!" cried Winifred. "He's going for my book!"

Max dashed to the door and down the front steps, the spell book clutched to his chest. He could hear Allison calling to him, and he followed her voice down toward the street and through the property's front gate.

Inside the house, Mary and Sarah wailed.

"I'm dying," Sarah cried, her blond hair and red dress soaked and dripping. "I'm too pretty to die."

And yet they weren't dying. Winifred drew a palmful of water to her mouth and tasted it.

"Winnie!" shrieked Mary in warning.

"Shut up!" Winifred spat back. "It is but water."

Mary tasted a few drops for herself. "Most refreshing," she quipped.

Sarah extended her tongue. "It is!" she said, then tried to swallow as much as she could.

"You idiot," Winifred said to Mary. "The boy has tricked us, and he's stolen the book. After him!"

Before they left, Winifred rescued the Black Flame Candle and stuck it in a tall kitchen cupboard, safely away from the strange metal clouds in the ceiling that spilled rain all over her mother's furniture and carpet.

Then the Sanderson sisters ran through the old wood, as they had not done in three hundred years. They arrived at the front gate, and the three of them stopped, elbow to elbow.

"'Tis a black river," said Mary.

"Perhaps it is not too deep," said Sarah.

Winifred grabbed her roughly by the arm and flung her ahead of them. Sarah shrieked, leaping, but when her heels touched the ground they didn't fall through.

"'Tis firm!" she exclaimed, gathering her skirts and doing a skipping dance on the asphalt. "'Tis firm as stone."

"Why, it's a road," said Winifred, joining her sister.

Mary took a few careful steps to join them.

"Sisters," said Winifred, drawing attention back to herself as usual. "My book."

They began to walk down the road together but were interrupted by the keen of fire trucks and ambulances. Red and white lights flashed through the sky, lighting up the witches' faces.

The sisters screamed in fear and turned, desperate for the comfort of the wood.

CHAPTER 5

AX, ALLISON, and Dani took a long way through the wood that the cat seemed to know by heart. It led them weaving through trees, stitching over and under fallen branches and the leaning columns of half-rotted trunks.

In the distance, Max could hear the eerie whine of emergency vehicles, no doubt called by the sprinklers going off on what was still considered public property.

The group, still led by the cat, emerged at the edge of the road. He leaped off the curb without even looking, and Allison and Dani followed him without having to be asked.

"Whoa, whoa, whoa," Max said, pulling up short. "This is the graveyard."

"Yes, it's the graveyard," said the cat, as if Max were one of the most annoying people he'd ever met—and perhaps he was. "Witches can't step foot here."

Max looked at the girls and waved a deflated hand at the cat. "He talks," he said.

"At least he's not trying to electrocute us," said Dani, which Max thought was a fair point.

"Is this a Halloween thing?" asked Allison. "Did the Sandersons cast a spell on you?"

The cat slipped through the gate without deigning to answer. "Follow me!" he called. "Over here." He paused, waiting for Allison to pry open the gate. She did, and they filed through and into the abandoned graveyard. Max was careful to shut the gate after them. If there had been a lock, he would've bolted the thing and taken the key with him.

"I want to show you something," explained the cat, "to give you an idea of exactly what we're dealing with."

They threaded through the quiet trees of the graveyard. The tombstones weren't arranged in careful rows, as they were in most graveyards Max had seen. Instead, they appeared in clusters or alone in unexpected places. Some parts of the graveyard even looked more like a park, with benches and fountains and the occasional mausoleum.

They walked for what seemed a long time, until they arrived in a clearing. They stopped at a tombstone near the edge of the woods.

" 'William Butcherson'?" Max read, crouching near it.

"Billy Butcherson was Winnie's lover," said the cat, "but she found him sporting with her sister Sarah. So she poisoned him and sewed his mouth shut with a dull needle so he couldn't tell her secrets, even in death. Winifred always was the jealous type."

Allison looked at the cat in wonder. "You're Thackery Binx," she said.

"Yes."

"So the legends are true," she added.

He paused, perhaps unsure how to respond. "Well, follow me," he finally said, leading them deeper into the graveyard. "I want to show you something else."

"Teenagers again," grumbled one of the men who had arrived in the noisy red vehicle. A stream of such men had rushed into the Sanderson house, and now they were filing out in a more orderly fashion.

"Every year they break into that house and do something stupid," agreed the man walking back to the street with him. Water dripped from his helmet. The captain had made him climb up and fiddle with the sprinkler system when they found the house empty.

"I hate Halloween," said the first man.

Sarah, crouched in the bearberry bushes next to her sisters, bit her bottom lip as the two men walked by. She'd never been acquainted with a man who looked quite so dashing in suspenders and oversize trousers. She stretched her neck, risking being spotted to keep the gentlemen in her line of sight a little longer.

"Who—who—who are they?" stuttered Mary, ducking farther into the bushes as if she could balance out her sister's derring-do.

"Boys," said Sarah wistfully.

"Perhaps they are the keepers of Master's red vessel?" Mary asked hopefully, eyeing the vehicle at the bottom of the road. A contraption near the top threw off red-and-white sparks. "His demon drivers?"

"They are witch hunters," corrected Winifred, sounding disgusted. "Observe," she added, "they wear black robes and carry axes to chop the wood to burn us."

Mary made a frightened sound. "Hold me?" she asked, snuggling her red-haired sister.

Winifred batted her away.

Sarah, meanwhile, was snacking on a spider she'd discovered on a nearby vine.

"Sisters," hissed Winifred. "Let me make one thing perfectly clear." The fiery vehicle had refilled with the witch hunters and tore away. "The magic that brought us back only works tonight, on All Hallows' Eve," said Winifred, getting to her feet and brushing off her skirts. "When the sun comes up, we're dust."

"Dust?" asked Mary.

"Toast."

"Toast?"

Winifred turned to her two sisters. "Pudding!" she shouted, throwing up her hands.

Mary shrieked, and Sarah shuddered then leaned toward Mary and whispered, "Do we like pudding?"

"Fortunately," said Winifred, looking off into the moonlit woods, "the potion I brewed the night we were hanged would keep us alive and young forever."

Sarah beamed and hopped excitedly.

"Unfortunately," trilled Winifred, turning on her heel and pushing past her sisters toward the sagging porch, "the recipe for that potion is in my spell book, and the little wretches have stolen it. Therefore, it stands to reason—does it not, sisters dear—that we must find the book, brew the potion, and suck the lives out of the children of Salem before sunrise. Otherwise, it's curtains. We evaporate! We cease to exist!" She gave each of them an accusing look. "Does thou comprehend?"

"Well, you explained it beautifully, Winnie," Mary rushed to say. "The way you sort of started out with the adventure part, and then you sort of slowly went into the—"

"Explained what?" asked Sarah.

Winifred pursed her lips and then seemed to make up her mind. "Come!" she shouted, shoving open the door of the house. "We fly."

Eventually, Binx took Max, Allison, and Dani to a small gravestone whose inscription was nearly invisible in the low light of the full moon. Max knelt to get a better look, running the tips of his fingers over letters and numerals time had sanded down. The gravestone marked the burial of a beloved daughter and sister who had died October 31, 1693. The name read: EMILY BINX.

"Because of me, my little sister's life was stolen," said Binx, studying the grave marker.

Max sat down, wrapping his arms around his knees. He could hear the wistfulness in Binx's voice. Max had never seen a cat look sad before, but Binx's expression was unmistakable, even with a muzzle and whiskers. Dani knelt down across from Max, and Allison perched on a weather-worn rock between the two of them, Winifred's spell book tucked safely in her lap.

"For years," said Binx, "I waited for my life to end so I could be reunited with my family, but Winifred's curse kept me alive. Then one day, I figured out what to do with my eternal life: I'd failed Emily, but I wouldn't fail again. When the three sisters returned, I'd be there to stop them. So for three centuries, I guarded their house on All Hallows' night, when I knew some airhead virgin might light that candle."

"Nice going, airhead," said Dani to her brother.

"Hey, look, I'm sorry, okay?" said Max, getting to his feet. He paused, then said hopefully, "We're talking about three ancient hags versus the twentieth century. How bad can it be?"

"Bad," said Binx.

Allison drew back the cover of Winifred's heavy spell book.

"Stay out of there!" shouted Binx.

Startled, Allison slammed it shut. "Why?" she asked, looking up.

"It holds Winifred's most dangerous spells," said Binx. "She must not get it."

Max grabbed the book from Allison and tossed it on the

ground. "Let's torch the sucker," he said, striking the silver lighter. He held it to the pages of the book, but the flame reared back as if a force field ensconced the thing.

"It's protected by magic," said Binx.

The sound of cackling broke the air and the group turned. The three Sanderson sisters hovered above them, each perched on a wood-handled broom. Sarah, on the left, wore a rich purple robe and a tight bodice the color of pressed wine grapes. Mary, on the right, was dressed in dowdier clothes, but they were the crimson of blood drops on snow. And Winifred, in the middle, wore forest green trimmed in faded gold.

"'It's just a bunch of hocus-pocus!'" Winifred quipped. "Sarah. Mary," she said, gesturing at her sisters. They veered off on their brooms in either direction.

Sarah went straight for Max. "Brave little virgin who lit the candle," she crooned, "I'll be thy friend."

Allison snatched up a dead branch and brandished it at the witch. "Hey!" she yelled. "Take a hike!"

The dried ends scraped at Sarah's skin and cloak and she winced and cried out, peeling away.

Winifred smiled at her book, still on the ground where Max had left it. "Book!" she called to it. The thing lifted off the ground and began to float toward her. "Come to Mummy!"

Binx leaped on top of it, and both he and the book clomped back to earth.

" 'Fraid not!" he called.

"Thackery Binx, thou mangy feline," Winifred said, sounding almost impressed. "Still alive?"

"And waiting for you," said Binx.

"Ah! Thou hast waited in vain. And thou will fail to save thy friends, just as thou failed to save thy sister." She pointed the end of her broom at him and dove.

"Grab the book!" shouted Binx.

Allison nabbed it, and the group bolted away from Winifred. They ran for the protection of the trees, but Mary cut them off, grinning as she bore down on them. They dodged her and she sailed past, no doubt circling to reassess.

Max pulled Dani close to him, sheltering her with one arm. "They can't touch us here, right?" he asked Binx.

"Well," said the cat, "*they* can't."

Dani turned to him. "I don't like the way you said that."

The Sanderson sisters, still perched on their brooms, reappeared out of the woods. Sarah licked her strawberry-colored lips. Winifred grinned widely and guided her broom closer to the three friends. Max realized that they'd returned to where they'd started—the grave of Billy Butcherson.

"Unfaithful lover long since dead," Winifred incanted, gesturing with unnaturally long knotted fingers, "deep asleep in thy wormy bed."

Allison clutched at Max's arm.

He wrapped his other arm tighter around Dani.

Her small fingers dug into his skin through his jacket.

"Wiggle thy toes," chanted Winifred, "open thine eyes, twist thy fingers toward the sky. Life is sweet, be not shy. On thy feet, so sayeth I!"

The ground began to tremble, and the earth over the nearby grave split, soil flying up as if it were boiling water. A coffin shivered out of the cut in the ground.

"Max," Dani whimpered. "Max."

He pulled her away from the grave. His pulse pounded in his ears and his whole body went slick with sweat.

The coffin lid burst open and a corpse dragged its way out. He grunted, shaking earth from his matted hair.

That's when he spotted Max, Allison, and Dani, who were watching him with horror. Billy Butcherson jumped, startled by their presence. The kids screamed and rushed away.

Billy looked around, confused, and spotted the gravestone behind him. He sighed.

"Hello, Billy," Sarah said, waving.

He smiled through the stitches keeping his lips sealed tightly shut.

"Catch those children!" shouted Winifred. "Get up! Get up! Get out of that ditch!" Billy pushed himself out of the broken bits of his final resting place. "Faster!"

Binx led his human companions through the woods, ducking under fallen branches and weaving between various tombstones and mausoleums. "In here," Binx said, stopping near what looked like a storm drain.

Allison helped Dani slip through first and then jumped in herself. Max spotted Billy Butcherson scrambling through the woods and grabbed a nearby branch, dragging it back as far as he could. When Billy was close enough, Max released the branch and it flew forward, knocking Billy's head from his shoulders.

Max whooped, but the headless body started toward him again and Max hurried into the drain.

Allison helped him to his feet at the bottom.

Dani stood nearby, coughing hard.

"You okay?" Allison asked her.

Dani grunted.

Allison handed the Sandersons' spell book to Max.

"What is this place, Binx?" Max asked, tucking the book under one arm.

"It's the old Salem crypt," Binx replied. "It connects to the sewer and up to the street."

"Charming," Allison said wryly.

"We need to find my parents," said Max. "They'll know what to do."

"Your parents?" asked Binx skeptically. "Adults always show up too late."

"Max is right," said Dani. "Mom fixes everything."

Binx seemed to take Dani's word more seriously than Max's.

He thought about it for a moment, then shrugged. "We might as well try," he said. "I don't have a better idea."

"They're at Town Hall," said Max. "Can you take us there?"

The cat gave him a look as if to say, *Am I an immortal cat who's been living in the same town for three hundred years?*

Just then, Max noticed a skeleton suspended from the vault's high ceiling. "Uh, don't look up, Dani," he said.

"Don't worry," she replied. Her eyes had been steadfastly focused on the ground since they'd arrived. "I won't."

"Relax," Binx told them. "I've hunted mice down here for years."

"Mice?" groaned Dani. "Oh, god."

But they had to choose between that and an undead colonist with a mandate to capture them, so rodents it would be.

CHAPTER 6

INIFRED GROANED when she saw her reanimated ex scrounging in the dirt to find his own head.

"Ah, crust," she said. "He's lost his head." She launched herself and her broom into a tight, angry circle. "Damn that Thackery Binx!" she cried. "Damn him!"

Beneath her, Billy bleated through his mouth stitches.

"Which way did they go?" Winifred asked, guiding herself closer to him.

He couldn't speak, of course, but he didn't point the way, either. She realized he must have gotten directionally confused when his skull went spinning. She looked around the graveyard and noticed a tunnel entrance partially hidden by climbing vines. The twigs around it were broken as if they'd been repeatedly trodden on.

"Billy," she snapped, turning back to his desiccated corpse. "Listen to me." His skin and spine crackled and popped as he forced his head back onto his body. "Follow those children, you maggot museum, and get my book. Then come find us; we'll be ready for them." She drifted backward, offended by the intensity of the dislike in his eyes. "Quit staring at me. Get moving down that hole." With that, she led her sisters back over the graveyard fence, muttering "Damn. Double damn!"

Winifred landed lightly on the walk beyond the graveyard gate. In the distance she could see the bell tower of the small graveyard chapel, its delicate lines and single bell outlined white by the pale moon.

As Winifred hurried to the fence, she felt a shock of remembrance from having walked that precise path before. She'd stood there and clutched the gate and watched a graveyard wedding take place more than three hundred years before—had watched another Sanderson say her vows in the only place where Winifred and her sisters didn't dare intervene.

"They're here," Winifred said. She could've meant the

children, or she could've meant the wedding party. For a moment, even Winifred wasn't sure.

The fence was wrapped with tendrils of dead and dying English ivy, and as she pressed her fingertips to the rough bodies of the vines, she imagined her own mortality and shuddered. It brought her back to the year 1993 and to the task very much at hand. "The children," she said, her voice gaining strength. "And that flea-riddled cat. I know they're here, but where are they?" She turned her face toward her brunet sister. "Sniff them out, Mary." She ignored Sarah entirely, who had started to climb the gate—but to what end, if they could not step foot on hallowed ground?

Mary clenched her fists and breathed deeply. "They're, they're . . ." She pressed her face against the iron bars and gave a plaintive sigh. "Oh, I can't. They've gone too far. I've lost them."

Winifred snatched the lobe of Mary's left ear and dragged her away from the fence. "I'll have your guts for garters, girl," she said, shoving her sister away. "Confound you!" Mary clutched at her aching ear, sniveling. "Very well," said Winifred, almost to herself, "we must outwit them. When Billy the butcher gets here with my book, we shall be ready for them." She turned back to her third sister. "Sarah! Let us start collecting children."

"Why?" asked Mary softly.

"Because, you great buffoon," Winifred said, wondering why the Devil had cursed her mother with so many senseless off-spring, "we want to live forever, not just until tomorrow. The more children we snatch, the longer we live."

"Right," Sarah said brightly, pointing at Mary. "Let us fly."

"Fly!" agreed Winifred.

"Wait," Mary said, causing the other two Sandersons to turn. "I have an idea." She plucked the brooms from her sisters' hands. "Since this promises to be a most dire and stressful evening, I suggest we form a calming circle."

"I am calm!" said Winifred.

"Oh, Sister," Mary said gently. "Thou art not being honest with thyself, are we? Hmmm?" She leaned in, as she might to a little girl. "Come on. Give—gimme a smile."

Winifred allowed a bashful grimace and then hopped into place, starting the calming circle. Mary and Sarah followed suit, each placing a hand on Winifred's shoulders. It wasn't a real spell circle, perhaps, but it made Winifred's younger sisters happy— and on very rare occasions, that was magic enough.

Allison and Max let Binx lead the way through the dark, dripping tunnels that snaked beneath the streets of Salem. Dani did a better job of keeping up with him, perhaps because she knew he'd do a better job of catching any mice or rats than Max would.

When he decided his little sister and the sarcastic cat were out of earshot, Max cleared his throat. "So," he said, not daring to look at Allison, "about earlier. I want to apologize."

"For lighting the candle?"

"Um. No, but I'm sorry for that, too."

"For ignoring us when we said it was time to go?"

"Uhhh." Max scratched the back of his head awkwardly. "Yeah, sorry for that, too."

"For your Rico Suave stunt with the phone number?"

"I knew you were upset about that."

"I wasn't upset about it," Allison said. "Just embarrassed. For you. You know, you don't have to be someone you're not just to ask a girl out."

There it was, sitting between the two of them: the specter of Max asking Allison on a date. Because that's what the whole thing boiled down to, right? He'd been too chicken to catch her in the hallway, just the two of them, and tell her that he liked her and wanted to buy her ice cream, if she was okay with that idea. Instead, he'd escalated and escalated and now three undead witches had put Dani on a dinner menu.

Max knew it, but he didn't know how to answer Allison. He didn't know what to do to make things right.

"Yeah, I get that," he finally said. "But I guess I wanted to apologize for what Dani said earlier. About—well, about you. It was embarrassing, and I'm sorry she did that."

"What did she say about me?"

"About your costume. About your, uh." He stopped talking and gestured lamely at his chest.

"You mean how she told me you've talked about my boobs?"

Max blushed. "Yeah," he said in a small voice, thinking that he'd rather be lost in those tunnels and facing death by sewer alligators than having that conversation.

"You don't have to apologize for her," said Allison. "Dani didn't do anything wrong. You might want to apologize for yourself, though."

Max cleared his throat. "Yeah," he said, for what felt like the hundredth time. "I—uh. I am sorry. I was an idiot. Like, a total idiot. But I wanted to tell my friend back in California about you, and he got bored with me talking about other stuff, so I thought—" He cleared his throat again. "But yeah, it was dumb. And it was my fault, not his or Dani's. I do get that."

"Thanks," Allison said, uncrossing her arms. Max snuck a

look at her face and determined she meant it. "I appreciate it. It's just a little weird, you know?"

Their footsteps echoed lightly off the walls as they continued following Binx's shadowy lead. Up ahead, they heard Dani telling Binx something about space travel.

"I know," Max said. "And I do know you're so much more than your—um, bazookas."

Allison laughed aloud this time. The sound of it bounced along with their footsteps, making Max's heart flutter.

"So what other stuff?" she asked.

"Hmmm?"

"The other stuff your friend didn't want to hear about. What was it?"

Max wet his lips. He didn't really want to tell her such personal stuff, but then again it was about *her*, so it was hard to use that defense. Besides, he had already gotten in a mess by saying the wrong thing.

"Like, the vase you made in sculpture class last week was sick. All those dots of blue and white in the glaze? It was awesome. And when Nancy fell asleep in chemistry and you slipped her the answer when Mrs. Jackson called on her? That was really cool of you. I like that even though you're the best person in the class, you don't rub it in."

Allison smiled, eyes downturned as she carefully picked

her way around a pile of mushy leaves. "Yeah, well," she said, "Nancy's parents are getting divorced; she deserves a break. Also, I am *not* better at chem than everyone else. Charles is."

"Charles is just louder," said Max.

Allison tucked a lock of hair behind her ear. "You really noticed all of that stuff?"

"Yeah," said Max. "I hope it's not creepy."

She laughed again. "It's not," she said. "I like those things about me, too."

"I just like that you work so hard. I don't know what you want to be when we, you know, grow up or whatever. But you *are* going to be it, Allison. You don't give yourself any excuses. That's—well, it's attractive."

"Thanks," Allison said again. Max could hear her smile in that single, simple word.

He waited for her to acknowledge that he admitted he liked her, but she didn't—not directly. Instead, she said, "I like the way you treat Dani. You were a total idiot back there with the candle," she added quickly. "But I can tell how much you love her. You're more *you* when she's around. More humble. I like that."

"She's got a lot of dirt on me," he joked, shrugging. "Plus, she's smarter than I am, and she's eight. It's hard not to be humble."

At that, Allison grinned. "What I meant was, I wish you

acted around other people the way you act around her. It's a good look on you."

Max scrutinized Allison's face, but it was too dark to tell exactly what she was thinking. He opened his mouth to ask, but Binx's voice cut through the dark, making them both jump.

"Here we are!" called the cat. "Up and out!"

"Think soothing thoughts," said Mary in her most centered voice. The sisters grasped arms and leaned into one another, revolving in a slow circle. "Rabid bats," she suggested. "Black Death. Mummy's scorpion pie."

With that, they broke apart and arranged themselves in a line, each sister lifting her face to the full moon.

"Mother," they breathed in unison.

A massive vehicle rolled up and stopped right in front of them. A set of doors near the front folded open with a mechanical gasp.

Inside, a man, perhaps in his forties, perched on a tall seat behind a set of controls. He took a look at the sisters and gave them a lecherous grin. "Bubble, bubble," he said, "I'm in trouble."

Winifred blushed. "Tell me, friend, what is this contraption?"

"I call it"—he spit a wad of gum through the window beside him—"a bus."

Winifred stroked her cheek with a two-inch fingernail. "A bus," she repeated. "And its purpose?"

He opened his arms to welcome them in. "To convey gorgeous creatures such as yourselves to your most"—he paused, drawing a fisted hand toward his chest—"forbidden desires," he finished meaningfully.

Winifred giggled. "Well," she said. "Fancy." She glanced at her sisters and back at the swaggering driver. "We desire children," she said.

He laughed loudly at that. "Hey, that may take me a couple of tries, but I don't think there'll be a problem. Hop on up."

Winifred led the way, as was the Sanderson practice. Sarah sidled onto the driver's lap.

"How does it work?" she asked, planting two hands on the wheel in front of her.

"Oh, gumdrop," the driver said, "it's already working."

The door hissed shut and the bus trembled as it came back to life. He helped her guide it onto the road. Sarah squealed, clapping, and the bus veered into the opposite lane.

The driver sat up straighter and grabbed on to the wheel.

Sarah wrested it back for herself, and as she did, her head bobbed into his field of vision.

A black cat appeared in the middle of the road, as if out of nowhere, and Sarah gunned the accelerator.

The bus clanked, one set of wheels bucking up a couple of inches, and then dropped back into place and kept going.

"Whoa!" said the driver, peering around her shoulder. "Speed bump."

Sarah pressed the button in the middle of the wheel, delighting in the high-pitched toot of the bus's horn.

"Binx?" called Dani, distressed. Seconds before, Max had lifted off the manhole cover overhead and started to climb out of the drainage tunnels, but he had ducked back down, shouting "Look out!"

Now the cat was nowhere to be seen.

Max hurried to push the heavy metal disc off again. He pulled himself up and then helped Dani and Allison climb out, too.

"Oh my god," Max said when he spotted Binx's flattened body in the middle of the road. He didn't react quickly enough to block Dani from seeing.

She cried out and buried her face in Allison's sweater. "No . . ." she sobbed.

"It's all my fault," Max said, starting to pace.

Allison took his wrist. "Max, it's not your fault," she said.

Dani grabbed on to his sleeve. "Look!" she said.

The three of them watched, amazed, as Binx's sides inflated like a balloon, as if he were taking a very deep breath. There was the sound of air filling desperate lungs and the soft snap of bones realigning.

Binx rolled over and looked up at them, shaking his head as if to clear it. "I hate it when that happens," he said.

Max, Allison, and Dani exchanged looks.

"What?" said Binx, bowing into a stretch. "I told you: I can't die." He took a step toward Dani. "Are you all right?" he asked, studying her small face.

CHAPTER 6

She nodded energetically. "Yeah," she said with a tear-streaked smile.

He darted over to bat at her shoelaces. When she giggled, he took a step back, seemingly satisfied. "Okay," he said, his yellow eyes peering into her pale green ones. "Then let's go find your parents."

CHAPTER 7

INIFRED AND Mary sat across the aisle from each other at the back of the bus, ignoring their sister Sarah's shenanigans. Outside, creatures milled about, going from house to house in the strangest clothes.

Mary leaped to her feet. "Stop!" she yelled.

The bus screeched to a halt and everyone turned to her.

"I smell children," she said, grinning.

"Marvelous," said Winifred, standing, as well.

Sarah hopped off the driver's lap and hurried toward them.

"Hey, cupcake," the driver said, grabbing her arm. "Don't I get your phone number? Your area code? You want my route schedule?"

Sarah simpered. "Oh," she said, batting a hand as if suddenly shy. "Thou wouldst hate me in the morning."

"No, I wouldn'tst!" he insisted.

Winifred gathered up her satin skirts and hurried to Sarah's side. "Oh, believe me," she said to the man, "thou wouldst." She extracted Sarah's arm from his grip and gave him a warning look.

"Party pooper," he grumbled.

Winifred turned up her nose at him and led her sisters off the bus.

Ahead of them stood a small house whose yard billowed with crimson smoke. Pitchforks jutted out of the soil.

"What is this, sisters?" Winifred asked, eyeing a short figure in a plush turtle body. It waved and scuttled off. In fact, creatures wove past the sisters from all directions, ducking and dodging and giggling as they crisscrossed the road. They were unlike any of the creatures Winifred had seen during her three hundred years in Hell—but then again, her own circle of reference had been somewhat limited and rather monstrous. Simple ghouls and goblins served as waitstaff in Lord Satan's palace, and the Sandersons had never received an invitation. Instead, they'd whiled away their hours with the likes of chupacabras and bunyips and terror beasts, and a towering black-caped man who never showed his face.

"What are those?" asked Mary, clutching Winifred's sleeve. She jumped at the sight of a small white figure with a smooth round head and the letters NASA tattooed over its heart. "What's that?"

"Um—" said Winifred. She tried to get a better look at the faces of the quick-moving fiends. "Hobgoblins," she said decisively.

A miniature angel glided over and curtsied, gold wings bobbing. "Bless you," she said sweetly.

The sisters shrieked and shrank back as she dashed away.

"Enough," Winifred said, catching her breath.

Mary trembled as she looked around. "Oh, sisters," she fussed, "I'm very confused. I smell children, but I don't see children." She gave a plaintive cry. "I've lost my powers!"

"Enough, enough," Winifred repeated, slapping her gently on each side of her face.

"Sorry," Mary said with a sniffle.

"We are witches," Winifred insisted. "We are evil. What would Mother say if she could see us like this?"

The three witches lifted their brooms toward the eastern sky and said, in unison, "Mother."

A sharp, high laugh broke through the night.

The witches turned and saw an old man clad in red, white hair settled in wisps about his ears.

"Master!" they cried. One by one, the sisters deposited their brooms at his gate, propping the handles against the slats of a pristine white fence, and hurried over, bowing and scraping at his doorstep.

"What kind of costumes are these?" the man asked.

The witches bowed deeply, arms extended. Even in Hell, they'd only seen Lord Satan from afar, when he passed through on a black chariot to survey his domain.

"It's the Sanderson sisters, right?" he asked.

The sisters simpered and clapped.

"At your service," Winifred said.

"Haven't seen you for centuries," said Satan, which made Winifred blush because she hadn't thought he would remember their first and heretofore only meeting, when she'd pledged herself to the sisterhood of red witches and received her spell book. "Why don't you come in?" he asked, waving them through the door.

They assembled in the main room of the house, which was surprisingly homey and cluttered.

"I want you to meet the little woman," Satan told the Sandersons.

"He has a little woman?" Winifred whispered to Mary.

"Sounds tasty," she replied.

The man leaned over a plush chair to speak to a woman whose face was hidden by a table lantern.

"Petunia face."

"What?" she snapped.

"We have company."

"I don't care who—" She sat up and the Sandersons gasped at the colorful twists wrapped through her curls.

"Sisters," Mary whispered, "Satan has married Medusa. See the snakes in her hair?"

The woman snarled at the sisters, who stepped back, fearful of waking her snakes.

"My three favorite witches," said Satan.

"Aren't you broads a little old to be trick-or-treating?" asked Medusa.

"We'll be younger in the morning," Winifred told her.

The woman snorted. "Yeah, sure," she said. "Me too." She left her drink on a nearby table and retreated up the staircase.

Winifred wandered into another room and let out a delighted sound when she found Satan's torture devices—wooden mallets and knives arranged along a metal strip for ease of access. There were two circles of fire, as well: one boiling a pot of water and another that seemed to be cooking sugared mud.

Winifred returned to the main part of the house just as Satan's wife came back down the stairs. They both laid eyes on Sarah, who was dancing slowly with the Devil.

"Master," she said softly.

With that, the woman of the house made the lights brighter and stormed down the stairs. "Okay, that's it," she snapped. "Party's over."

Sarah broke away from her dance, and Mary sat up quickly from the comfortable chair where she'd been experimenting with the box the woman had been observing. It seemed to transport the watcher to another world. In the box, a small dog had scuttled across polished wood floors, and Mary had laughed and shouted, ducking and turning her own body to help it avoid obstacles.

"Get out of my house," said the woman.

"Pudding face," her husband pleaded, approaching her.

"Shove it, Satan," she snapped.

"Oh," said Sarah seriously. "Thou should not speak to Master in such a manner."

"They call me Master," the man said, pleased.

"Wait till you see what I'm gonna call you," said his wife. She threw some brightly colored bags at the sisters. "Take your Clark Bars and get outta my house."

Winifred stalked forward, putting herself between her sisters and the pale, tired-looking woman. "Make us," she said.

"Honeybunch," said the old man.

"Ralph," the woman said sharply, "sic 'em." A small furry demon leaped up and chased the sisters from the house.

The demon stopped at the doorstep and trotted back inside. The sisters ran the rest of the way to the road, where they paused to catch their breaths.

"My broom!" Sarah cried, realizing it had gone missing.

"My broom!" echoed Mary.

"My broom," Winifred huffed. "Purloined. Curses."

They started down the road on foot. "Sisters, look," said Mary, holding up a candy bar she'd taken from the house. "'Tis the chocolate-covered finger of a man named Clark." She bit into it. "Mmmm—ew—" She spat it out. "It's candy," she said, aghast. "Why would the master give us candy?"

"Because he is not our master," said Winifred sharply.

"He isn't?"

"And these are not hobgoblins," Winifred added. She tore the mask from a passing creature, revealing the startled face of a small blond boy. "See?" she said, gesturing.

"Cool it, man!" cried the boy.

Mary touched his arm. "A child," she said hungrily.

The boy hit her with a bulging fabric sack. "Weirdos!" he shouted as he ran away.

"Weirdos?" repeated Sarah.

"Sisters," said Winifred, "All Hallows' Eve has become a night of frolic. Where children wear costumes and run amok."

"Amok," chorused Sarah. "Amok, amok, amok, amok, a—"

Winifred elbowed her in the stomach and Sarah doubled over, clutching her abdomen.

"Oh, Winnie," pleaded Mary. "Just one child."

"We haven't the time, Sister," said Winifred. "We must find my book. Then thou may have as many children as thou desires."

Mary hummed. "Boiled and toasted and sautéed and roasted and—"

"Yes, yes," Winifred interrupted, knitting her fingers together eagerly. "But first, the book."

CHAPTER 8

T LAST, Max and the girls homed in on Salem's Town Hall, a two-story red-brick building with the sound of a live band spilling out and down the street. The windows of the second floor were washed with purple light from the party happening inside, and a banner above the double doors read SALEM'S 16TH ANNUAL TOWN HALL PUMPKIN BALL.

"Oh, great," Max said, leading the group across the street. "How are we ever gonna find Mom and Dad in this place?"

"I'll wait outside," said Binx, jumping into the low branches of a nearby tree. "If anything happens, shout for me."

Max eyed the noisy building. "How will you hear us?" he asked.

"I won't," said Binx. "But it might help you feel better."

Dani held out her arms and Binx relented, leaping into them. Max jogged up the steps to open the door for Allison and Dani.

"I should be eating Peanut M&Ms right now," Dani muttered as she stalked past.

"Actually," said Max, "you should be in bed."

She rolled her eyes. "I'm going to find Mom," she called to Max before disappearing between a policewoman and a jellyfish.

Town Hall's second floor was a huge ballroom, and it was packed with half the adults in Salem. On the raised stage, a skeleton in a top hat sang Sinatra's "Witchcraft." The band members were dressed as skeletons, too, and they really blasted the brass. Max wondered, fleetingly, whether their drummer would give him lessons.

The whole audience was dressed up, and they seemed to have gone all out. Max spotted a sequined Viking, a knight in a full suit of silver armor, and a timely Bill Clinton.

"Are you sure your parents can fix this?" Allison shouted over the music. "What if they don't believe us?"

"What choice do we have?" said Max.

Two strong hands grabbed Max by the shoulders, and he shouted, spinning around. "Oh," he said, relieved, "Dad."

"It's not Dad," said his father in a forced Romanian accent. "It's *Dadula*."

Max winced at the terrible joke.

"Oh, my goodness," his dad said, taking Allison by the hand, "who must this charming young blood donor be?"

"Dad!" Max snapped. "Something terrible happened."

"Dani?" his dad asked immediately, letting go of Allison. "What's wrong? What—"

"No," said Max, "Dani's fine."

His dad's face grew stern. "Good," he said, then turned to Allison and excused himself. He put his arm around Max's shoulders and pulled him off to the side. "What is it?"

"It's—it's complicated, okay? Promise you'll believe me."

"You know I can't do that in advance. Shoot, Max. Look, whatever it is, just tell me."

Onstage, the skeleton did a complicated dance turn and leaned into his microphone: "'Cause it's witchcraft, that crazy witchcraft."

Across the room, Dani sidestepped a costume that made the wearer look like Aladdin seated on a flying carpet. She peered into the mouth of an alligator. "Mom?" she asked hopefully. The reptile shook its head and waddled off.

She turned and nearly crashed into a blond woman in a red bustier, the cups of which were built out into two spiraled cones.

"Mom?" Dani asked, aghast. She nearly dropped Binx. "What are you supposed to be?"

Her mother looked flustered. "Madonna," she said, and

gestured to her costume. "Well, you know," she continued, suddenly self-conscious. "Obviously. Don't you think?"

Dani sighed. "Come here," she said, holding Binx out toward her mother in hopes that he would speak.

"What?" asked her mom, crouching to hear her daughter better.

Dani pointed to Binx's head with one hand. "This cat, okay?" she said. "He can talk. My brother's a virgin. He lit the Black Flame Candle. The witches are back from the dead, and they're after us." She took a breath. "We need help."

Her mom paused and then placed a worried hand on Dani's cheek. "How much candy have you had, honey?"

The words came tumbling out of Dani as she realized that her parents might actually not believe her: "Mom, I haven't OD'd. I haven't even had a piece. They're real witches, they can fly, and they're gonna eat all the kids in Salem. They're real."

"All right," her mother said warily. "Let's . . . just . . . find your father."

The jazzy skeleton wrapped up his crooning. "Thank you, ghouls and ghoul-ettes!" he said to the crowd, grinning as the applause swelled and died down again. The band immediately began an up-tempo cover of Jay Hawkins's "I Put a Spell on You."

The Dennison family convened, with Allison looking on from the sidelines.

"Guys," Mr. Dennison said impatiently, "I love you, but enough is enough. Just calm down."

Max fumed. "But they're gonna come—"

"Don't you see how crazy this sounds?" insisted his dad.

Dani caught sight of something across the room. "Max!" she shouted. "Max! They're here!"

Max turned away from his dad. His eyes rippled over the crowd. When he spotted the three witches—Winifred apparently chewing out Mary and Sarah sucking face with a mummy—Max took off. He ignored his parents' pleas for him to come back and instead scrambled onto the stage. He wrestled the microphone from the skeleton.

"Cut the music!" he shouted.

"Hey, man, I'm in the middle of a song," complained the singer.

"It's an emergency," Max told him, still speaking into the mic. "Only for a minute." He turned to face the crowd. "Will everybody listen up, please? Your kids are in danger."

The crowd gasped, and startled adults pressed closer to the stage.

"Three hundred years ago," said Max, "the Sanderson sisters bewitched people, and now they've returned from their grave."

The roomful of people laughed.

"Hey, I'm serious," Max insisted. "It's not a joke. I know this sounds dumb, but they're here tonight. They're right over there," he added, pointing to where the sisters stood, each of them look-ing nervous.

A spotlight scanned the crowd and stopped on the three Sandersons, and everyone gasped again, stepping away from them.

Winifred recovered the fastest. "Thank you, Max," she said, tapping her long fingernails against her chin, "for that marvelous introduction."

The crowd laughed, and this time a smattering of applause also washed through the room.

"I put a spell on you," she said dramatically, throwing her hands in the air. The keyboardist took this as a cue and began to play a fizzy, sparkling tune. "And now you're mine," said Winifred with a mischievous smile.

Max heard Dani shout above the appreciative murmurs: "Don't listen to them!" She was right, he knew. What if the witches decided to *actually* put a spell on everyone? He leaped off the stage to help his sister as their parents dragged her toward the exit. Allison trailed helplessly behind them, trying to reason with Max's mom without being disrespectful.

"You can't stop the things I do," said Winifred, then broke into a trill: "I ain't lyin'." She pirouetted to scattered giggling. "It's been three hundred years, right down to the day. Now the witch is back, and there's hell to pay. I put a spell on you," she repeated, working the crowd and making her way to the stage, then breaking into full-throated song: *"And now—you're miiiine!"*

The snare drum rolled and the brass flared. "Hello, Salem!" she called, smirking at the children's attempt to warn the parents. "My name's Winifred! What's yours?" She sashayed to the edge of the stage. *"I put a spell on you, and now you're gone!"*

"Gone, gone, gone!" sang her sisters, taking over the two mics reserved for backup singers. *"So long!"*

"My whammy fell on you," crooned Winifred, *"and it was strong."*

"So strong," sang Sarah and Mary, *"so strong, so strong!"*

"Your wretched little lives have all been cursed," sang Winifred, grinning when the audience cheered. *"'Cause of all the witches working, I'm the worst! I put a spell on you—and now you're mine."*

Max and Dani's parents deposited the kids near the front door.

"Take your sister home," said Max's dad. "It's too late for pranks." He took his wife by the hand and led her back into the crowd.

Max, Allison, and Dani didn't head downstairs right away. Instead, they watched in horror as the whole ballroom danced to the witches' song.

Someone bumped into Max and he turned, ducking when he saw Billy Butcherson stumbling toward them through the delighted crowd. Dani screamed and grabbed Allison, dragging her in the other direction.

"*If you don't believe, you better get superstitious,*" sang Winifred, having the time of her life. "*Ask my sisters—*"

"*Oooh, she's vicious!*" they chorused.

"*I put a spell on you!*" belted Winifred. "*I put a spell on you!*"

Mary and Sarah joined her, and the three of them began to dance toward the crowd. "*Ah say ento pi alpha mabi upendi,*" they chanted.

"*Ah say ento pi alpha mabi upendi!*" repeated the crowd.

Max suddenly felt lightheaded, and the air seemed to fill with the smells of fresh-baked cookies and brownies.

"It's a spell!" Max shouted, pressing his palms to his ears. "Don't listen!"

Dani and Allison followed his example, but the adults within earshot ignored him.

"*In comma coriyama—*" sang the witches onstage.

"*In comma coriyama!*" the adults crowed back.

"*Hey—*"

"*Hey!*"

"*Hi—*"

"*Hi!*"

"*Say bye-byyyyyye!*" Winifred belted out, waving dramatically at the crowd, then added, with a smirk: "Bye-bye!"

The crowd roared and whistled as the lights cut to a crimson wash.

As the band struck up the next song, Winifred could be heard cackling as she sealed the curse: "Dance, dance, dance until you die!" Sarah pranced off the stage after her, swinging her skirts.

"Good work, Winnie," said Mary, catching up to them.

"Of course it was," said Winifred. From behind the velvet stage curtains, she watched the result of her dirty work. "Now these silly parents will be occupied without a thought for their darling children at home in their darling beds. We will have a feast tonight, sisters! But first, we must find my book."

The kids ran down the block and into an alleyway behind Allegra's, one of Salem's most popular restaurants. The alley was filled with stinking trash cans and discarded kitchen equipment—including an industrial oven and some broken blenders—waiting to be hauled away.

Max kicked the oven, cursing. He only managed to hurt his foot, so he limped back and leaned against the closest brick wall. "This is really bad!" he shouted.

"Max, come on," said Allison, startled. "Calm down."

"Look," he snapped, "I want you to take Dani back to your house and don't let her out of your sight."

"Max, I'm not leaving you," said Dani.

The restaurant door crashed open, and Max, Dani, and Allison ducked behind the piles of trash. A chef stepped out to pick a lobster out of the fish tank. Just as the door swung shut behind him again, Binx's eyes widened. "Uh-oh," he said, and jumped down to share the kids' hiding place.

The three witches strolled up, following Mary, who sniffed loudly as she walked.

"I smell . . ." she muttered, tasting the air. "Winnie, I smell . . . I smell . . ." She paused. "Scrod." She withered under Winifred's hateful look. "It's a bottom dweller," she explained. "You know, you can eat it sometimes with lovely bread crumbs, a little bit of margarine. Oooh—or olive oil is good." She began to stutter and devolve from nerves.

Winifred gave a disgusted sniff in her direction and abandoned the alley, but Sarah stepped toward the trash cans, her blue eyes wide as she searched for the source of some feeling she couldn't quite put her finger on.

"Sarah," Winifred said shrilly, though she didn't bother to wait for her. "Sarah!"

As Allison tried to inch past the oven, its door fell open and blocked her way. She reached for the handle to close it, then paused and turned to Max with a conniving smile. "I have an idea," she said.

Mary and Sarah followed Winifred through town, toward a slender ironwork gate. Behind the gate was the largest building the witches had ever seen, its dark windows peering out of red-brick walls. They'd come because of the smell, which was strong enough that even Winifred, whose sense of smell was poor, had caught it as the wind switched.

"What is this place?" breathed Sarah.

"It reeks of children," Mary said, almost humming in delight.

"It is a prison for children," explained Winifred. She opened the creaking front gate and let in her sisters, then cast a spell to unlock the prison's heavy front door. Above the door, tall white letters spelled the words JACOB BAILEY HIGH SCHOOL.

The hallway was wide and quiet when the sisters crept in—wider than the river that once ran through town, and quieter than the nights when they went down to it to fish out dead fish and fishermen.

As they shut the door behind them, the place filled with an unholy howl. "Welcome to high school hell," said a dark and warbling voice. "I'm your host, Boris Karloff Jr." This announcement was punctuated by a thunderous crash and a crescendo of evil laughter. The sisters wove from one side of the hall to the

other, trying to determine where the sound was coming from and how to avoid its owner.

"It's time to meet our three contestants," the disembodied voice continued. "Sarah, Mary, and Winifred Sanderson. Read any good spell books lately?"

The sleek, dark body of Thackery Binx flickered through an open door. He hissed at the sisters and scampered off.

Winifred began to lead her sisters toward him when a pleasant female voice said, "Hello, welcome to the library. *Bonjour, bienvenue a la bibliothéque.*"

The sisters looked at one another and then shuffled into the dark room and down a narrow hall. They found themselves in a distant wing, where strange carvings sat on narrow white pedestals.

"I would like a book," the woman said. "*Je voudrais un livre.*" Her voice came from within a small room lined with metal. The sisters slipped past the iconography and into the room, which smelled strongly of burnt clay and children. The sisters grinned at one another, then looked for the source of the voice and the smell. A black box with a red blinking light sat on one shelf. The woman repeated her last request, but her voice filtered through the mesh paneling of the box.

"I think she's trapped inside," said Mary, sounding sorry for her.

Winifred's eyes fell to the floor, where mounds of clothes—socks and sleeveless tops and shorts in coordinating colors—lay scattered.

"It's a trap," she said, but before she could turn, the heavy metal door swung shut. Even before she saw the girl's face through the window, she knew that she and her sisters were toast.

CHAPTER 8

Winifred reached for Sarah's arm. She was more afraid than she had been three hundred years before, on the night she'd gotten them caught by the townspeople. Then as now, it was because of things she hadn't bothered to do. Her mother would have been so angry at her, were she there. She'd have criticized her and told her she should be more thorough, more thoughtful. More like—

There was a click, and the room grew warm enough to make Winifred sweat.

She muttered spells beneath her breath—every spell she could remember, in fact—spells of protection and revenge, spells for clearing storms and finding a lost pair of spectacles.

The three children—and even that damned cat, who looked awfully pleased with himself—peered through the narrow window of the box.

Winifred's hair began to smoke and then alighted, and so, too, did the lace hem of her dress, and then she yelled "Wretches!" and she and her sisters burst into flames.

CHAPTER 9

 **LLISON WANTED** to check the kiln for debris, but Max worried that seeking the witches' smoking bodies would scar Dani for life. Instead, the two of them decided to put the kiln on a longer second cycle, hoping that the Sandersons would have mostly turned to ash by morning. They'd sneak back in the next day or Sunday to clean it out, and by Monday morning no one would have any idea what had happened in the arts wing.

Max turned to Dani, then, who had moved away from the kiln door when the witches started to burn. She held Binx close to her, petting him and kissing the top of his head.

"It's done," Max said to her, and when the words sank in, Dani beamed up at him.

"Really?"

He ran over and scooped her up, spinning her around and nearly knocking over an unfired ceramic skull that someone had made.

"Really," he said softly against the side of his little sister's head. His own body relaxed, then, as all the adrenaline seemed to pour out of it.

Allison walked over and put one hand on each of his shoulders, which sent butterflies careening through his digestive system.

"Let's get home," she said. She was looking at Dani, but it sent a happy shiver down Max's spine.

Allison took Max's hand when he set Dani down, and they all slipped out of the school, breaking into a run as they neared the ironwork gates. Dani whooped, and the sound of her celebrating made it all feel real to Max, too.

"Farewell, Winifred Sanderson!" shouted Binx, leaping from Dani's arms to the rain-slicked street and racing about not unlike a dog after its own tail.

Max grabbed Allison around the waist, spinning her, and then set her down and gave Dani a big kiss on the cheek. Dani squealed but didn't push him away. Instead she grabbed his face and kissed his forehead, grinning.

Binx dashed away, leading the jubilant kids down the block. Leaves fell around them like confetti in oranges and browns and golds. They crossed into a park, and Allison took off after Dani, toward a grassy field where Dani could show off her handstands and cartwheels.

Max relaxed against the park fence and looked up at Binx, who had settled onto the nearby branch of an oak tree. "We did it, Binx," he said, grinning. "We stopped them."

"I've wanted to do that for three hundred years," Binx said thoughtfully. He paused and then added, "Ever since they took Emily."

Max's smile faded into a serious look. He turned to face Binx, who was silhouetted against the opalescent moon. "You really miss her, don't you?" he asked.

Binx looked away without answering, but Max could see the pain and self-loathing knitted across his small furry face.

"Man, you can't keep blaming yourself for that," Max said. "That happened so long ago."

Binx's narrow shoulders shifted up in a small shrug. "Take good care of Dani, Max," he said. "You'll never know how precious she is until you lose her." He leaped out of the tree and headed across the park, slipping into the shadows.

"Hey, Binx!" called Max, straightening. The cat turned and looked at him. His eyes seemed to glow yellow in the low light. "Where do you think you're going?" Max asked, walking toward him. "You're a Dennison now, buddy. One of us."

"Come on, Binx!" Dani called from the clearing. "Let's go home."

"Home," Binx repeated wistfully. He glanced from Max to Dani and then scurried after her as she linked one arm through Allison's and headed back to the sidewalk.

As Max watched them saunter ahead of him, he thought about how he'd hated Salem as soon as his parents had announced their move—even before he knew anything about the town or their house or Allison Watts. "Home," he said. The word sounded weird to him, but it also sounded right.

Max caught up with the others and led the way home. He could tell that Dani was getting sleepy because she kept repeating herself, and because her eyes stayed closed a little too long when she blinked.

He took her hand as they passed by Town Hall, where the Pumpkin Ball was still going strong. The lead singer's vocals poured through the open door: "*Jump, magic, jump; dance, magic, dance. . . .*"

"Getting back into the kiln tomorrow's going to be easy," Allison said wryly. "All the adults are going to be asleep till lunchtime."

Max yawned into the crook of his arm. "That doesn't sound so bad," he said.

Allison smiled at him and shook her head.

When they reached the Dennison house, the lights inside were still out. Max unlocked the door as Dani checked the bowl of candy they'd left on the porch.

"Aw, man," she grumbled. "Only Almond Joys are left."

Allison patted her back reassuringly. "Don't worry; you can have whatever's left over at my house."

"Promise?"

"Only if your brother brings you over tomorrow," Allison said, smiling at Max.

Dani rolled her eyes. "There'd better be Twix bars if I'm covering for you two."

"Mom?" Max asked, leading the girls inside. "Dad?" He flipped on the light. His parents' coats were nowhere to be found. Nor were his mom's keys, which she always had trouble tracking down despite dropping them on the entry table each time she came home. His dad had left behind his Swiss Army knife, though, and Max plucked it up and pocketed it just in case. He had a feeling that after their night, he'd be paranoid of witches for the rest of his life.

"We got a new cat!" Dani said, pushing past him. "Mom?"

Max looked at Allison. "Well, I guess they're still partying," he said, stepping out of her way. "Come on in."

They went to Max's room, because Dani always liked to sleep there when she was anxious. She said that even monsters were afraid of the stink of teenage boys. Dani gave Binx a bowl of milk before slipping under Max's covers. "You're my kitty now," she said, petting Binx's head. "You'll have milk and tuna fish every day, and you'll only hunt mice for fun."

"You're going to turn me into one of those fat, useless contented house cats," Binx said.

Dani giggled. "You betcha."

Allison chuckled, watching them. She and Max were sitting on a pile of pillows near the staircase that led into the bedroom's loft. Allison grabbed a nearby blanket and wrapped it over her shoulders, then leaned into Max. He was sure the sudden acceleration of his heartbeat would startle her, but her breathing was soft and steady. He wrapped one arm around her gingerly, afraid to disturb her, and she pressed her cheek more firmly against his chest. He wanted to touch her hair but was afraid that might be too forward. Instead, he tucked his fingers around her elbow and thought about how he might ask her on their first proper date. Part of him still wanted to take her to the hill in the graveyard that overlooked the harbor, where he went to think, but after all they'd been through, it seemed a bit creepy. Maybe he'd take her to a movie, like Dani had suggested.

"You know, Binx," Dani said sleepily as the cat finished his milk and leaped up to snuggle into her arms, "I'll always take care of you. My children will take care of you, too. And their children after that, and theirs after that. Forever and ever . . ." She trailed off, and when Max looked over, he saw that she was fast asleep.

CHAPTER 9

In the cool October night, wisps of vapor the color of moss-green algae or fresh growth on old branches filtered across the moon's full face. The vapor slipped through low-hanging clouds but didn't become part of them, and after a few minutes the vapor began to fall back to earth, as if weighed down by the condensation that had begun to bead on grass blades and window glass.

It funneled down the chimney of Jacob Bailey High School's kiln, and when every last breath of it was inside the school, it whirled and churned and knocked down the reinforced metal door. Winifred strode out of the kiln, hacking and batting at the smoke still hanging in the air.

"Hello," she muttered testily, "I want my book. *Bonjour, je veux mon livre.*"

Her hair was even wilder and wirier than before—and the grin plastered on her face was murderous—but she otherwise looked just the same as when those bratty kids first trapped her. Her sisters followed her out of the broken kiln in similar condition, Sarah trying desperately to wipe black ash from her sleeves and skirts.

"Find them," Winifred ordered, turning on Mary.

"W-what?"

"The boy and that blasted girl," she said. "And that child with the wretched cat. They have my book and that book is our last chance to stay in this world. Find them."

"I—I don't know," stuttered Mary.

"You don't know?" said Winifred scornfully.

"Well, Winifred, everything smells like smoke now."

"What are you good for, then?" demanded Winifred.

"I—well—I don't know. I—I'm still your sister, Winnie." She quailed under the look Winifred gave her then. "Never mind!" she yelped. "I didn't mean it!"

Spinning away, Winifred swung angrily at the nearest sculpture, grabbing a cobalt blue vase and throwing it onto the concrete floor. The vase shattered into a dozen pieces. Winifred groaned. "Just find them," she said over her ash-dusted shoulder.

The night had gone quiet. It was so late that all the children of Salem were tucked into bed. So late, in fact, that their babysitters had fallen asleep, as well, drifting off as they waited for their employers to come back from the Town Hall Pumpkin Ball.

As a result, the town felt deserted and eerie beneath the harsh light of its own streetlamps.

Jay and Ernie didn't seem to notice, however.

Long-haired Jay perched on the hood of an old black sedan while stocky Ernie leaned against the front bumper, unwrapping fun-size candy bar after fun-size candy bar and stuffing himself silly. Toilet paper cascaded around them from the branches of a sycamore tree that had mostly shed its leaves for winter. The boys knew the local cops would unfairly presume them guilty if a stranger's house—or worse, a classmate's—ended up decked out this way, so instead they'd TP'd Jay's house. In the morning, his parents would just look disappointed and point them toward the stepladder.

"You wanna smash some pumpkins?" Jay asked, toying with a half-empty roll of toilet paper.

"No," said Ernie around a mouthful of chocolate.

"Well, then you wanna look in windows and watch babes undress?"

"It's three o'clock," Ernie said. "They're undressed already."

Jay flung the paper away. "Well then, you think of something."

"I don't feel so good."

"That's 'cause you're eating too much candy, you oinker," Jay said, smacking the latest bar from Ernie's hand. He hated when Ernie got this way—so fixated on one thing, and usually a thing that was totally boring and didn't involve Jay at all.

The witches saw the boys before the boys saw the witches.

Mary, who had been desperately sniffing the air for what felt like two hours but was probably merely minutes, was the most excited to spot them.

"The boy, Winnie!" she hissed, tugging on her redheaded sister's sleeve.

"Are you sure that's the right one?" Winifred asked.

Mary was not, but she knew that Winifred did not like insecurity.

"I am," she said. "It must be."

"It *must be*," said Winifred, "or it *is*?"

"It is!" Mary said with more conviction than she felt.

"Good," said Winifred. Her voice grew darker and more vindictive then: "The girl who trapped us in that fire box is mine. I'll teach her to try and burn a witch."

Jay and Ernie were, to an outside observer, old enough to be more men than boys, but the night was heading toward dawn and the Sanderson sisters were not eager to discriminate.

The witches crept up behind them. As they did, Sarah danced through the soft, waving curls of white paper, spinning and smiling.

Mary homed in on the strongest scent in the street: without a second thought, she pressed her nose against the larger boy's left foot.

"Yo, witch," Ernie said, smacking her with Max Dennison's nearly empty candy bag. "Get your face off my shoe."

Mary scuttled backward, fixing her hair. "Oh," she said, frightened more of Winifred than of this boy with the strange hair and the useless weapon. "Wrong boy. Oh, sorry, Winnie."

Sarah plucked up a scrap of toilet paper and swung it about, watching the thin material make exquisite shapes as it caught the air.

Winifred threw her hands up. "Why, why, why was I cursed with such idiot sisters?" she demanded.

Sarah did a little twirl. "Just lucky, I guess."

Mary snorted before she could stop herself, and Winifred let out a tearless sob.

The three sisters turned away to try to find their original targets.

"Oh, man," said Jay. "How come it's always the ugly chicks that stay out late?"

One by one, the Sandersons turned. Sarah in particular looked prepared to turn someone into a box turtle or slug. Something slow on the road and sweet on the tongue.

"*Chicks?*" prompted Winifred.

Winifred managed to bring the boys to their knees thanks to a particularly well-delivered lightning bolt. She gave them over to her sisters to drag back up the road to their house in the woods. Once there, she summoned two of her favorite cages from the closet. They'd once housed Winifred's prized phoenix twins— the ones Mary set free out of pity at the age of twelve.

Winifred was happy to have them empty now, for she shoved one boy into each cage and sealed the doors with iron locks. The cages crackled with electricity as she used her magic to rehang the huge iron things on their ceiling hooks. The impertinent boys wept and pled for pity without pause.

CHAPTER 9

Winifred ignored them. Their suffering would teach them not to disrespect their elders—even if they wouldn't have much time to live out that lesson. "We haven't much time left," she said. "We shall have to make the potion from memory."

"Let us outta here," whimpered the blond boy, who had told Sarah that his name was Jay.

"Yeah," said the other boy, who called himself Ernie. "We're really sorry."

"We think you're really cute," Jay added with effort, hoping to win them over.

"Hush!" snapped Winifred. She began to pace. "I can't think," she muttered to herself.

"Remember, remember," her two sisters chanted in low voices, trailing her across the room. She hated when they did that, but both were stupidly convinced that it worked. "Remember, Winnie, remember."

"Now I remember!" Winifred cried, whirling around.

Mary and Sarah gasped and jumped back.

"I was here," Winifred said, ignoring them. She pointed to where the podium stood. "The book was there. You, Mary—you were here."

Mary beamed at being remembered.

"Sarah, you were in the back," Winifred added, fluttering her hand dismissively. "Dancing, idiotically. And the book said—"

Mary leaned in. "Yes?"

"I remember it like it was yesterday," Winifred said, grinning.

"Yes?" said Mary.

"Oil of boil," Winifred recited, the long nail of her pointer finger dancing through the air as if reading a spell, "and a dead man's nose."

Jay and Ernie exchanged a suffering look. *Nose?* Ernie mouthed. Jay cringed. Is this why the old ladies had kidnapped them? To turn them into potion ingredients?

"Dead man's toes!" Sarah crowed.

"She's trying to concentrate," snapped Mary, shooing her away.

Sarah shrugged and wandered off, nibbling her lucky rat tail.

"No, his thumb," said Winifred softly.

"Thumb?" asked Mary.

Ernie chewed anxiously on his left thumbnail.

"Or was it his gums?" asked Winifred. "A dead man's buns . . . ?"

"Buns," said Mary. "Buns. Sounds like—"

"Mums?" asked Winifred hopefully.

"Mums. Funs . . . funs . . ."

"Chungs," said Winifred.

"Chungs?" Jay asked, turning to give Ernie a startled, anxious look.

Ernie drew a finger across his neck to make Jay shut up. "Dead man's chungs," he said breathlessly.

"No," said Mary. "There's no such thing as chungs."

Winifred made a helpless sound. "You're right."

"I am?" asked Mary. Then, with more certainty: "I'm right."

"It's no use," said Winifred. "I don't remember the ingredients. I—I—I've got to have my book!"

Behind her, Sarah grabbed the base of Jay's cage and spun it about, making him whimper and clutch at the hammered iron bars. She giggled.

Winifred went to the kitchen and retrieved the Black Flame Candle, which had been merrily flickering the whole night.

"Behold, sisters," she lamented. "The candle burns to a stub. Soon our time will be spent, and we will have wasted our last chance."

"Curtains," Mary whispered, finally putting together Winifred's earlier rant.

"My dress is made of curtains," Sarah said, before trading Jay's cage for Ernie's and twirling in the other direction.

Winifred stalked past both of her sisters and threw open the nearest window. She leaned out and released a high-pitched keen: "Booo-ooook!" Her shoulders sagged. "Come home," she pleaded. "Or make thyself known."

Mary petted her back as Winifred dissolved into a fit of sobs.

CHAPTER 10

LLISON BEGAN to stir, which woke Max from one of the deepest sleeps of his life.

"Hi," he said to her, unable to hide a smile.

She smiled back. "Hi," she said sheepishly. She picked up the clock near her hip. "Oh my god," she said. "It's five o'clock. My parents are gonna kill me. I should go." She leaped up and grabbed her sweater.

Max stretched. "I wish you could stay," he said.

Allison looked at him. At first a worried look passed over her face. She was unsure of what he meant and where he wanted this to go. But his dopey grin made her relax.

"Hey," Max said, straightening as he woke more fully and

realized she was worried not only about being out so late but about being out late with a boy. "We'll figure it out together, okay? You can say Dani got sick on sugar and I needed help. Dani will vouch for you. Plus, my parents saw us together out in public. They know we weren't—you know. . . ."

"Maybe I'll say the girls kidnapped me as a prank," Allison said thoughtfully.

Max nodded. Allison would know best, he realized, but it made him wonder if she didn't want her parents to know about him at all. Maybe he'd misread her again and she didn't really like him back. Or maybe she did, but she was embarrassed about him. He got to his feet and stuffed his hands into his pockets.

"I'll walk you back," he offered.

Allison glanced at Dani, who was still asleep. The dark curving line of a black cat was pressed against her cheek.

"Poor Binx," Allison said.

Max looked at him then, too. "Yeah, poor Binx," he said, thinking of their conversation at the park. He couldn't imagine being separated from his family for so long. Dani had meant well when she said a dozen generations of Dennisons would look after him, but Max knew that her promise wasn't much comfort to Thackery Binx.

"We owe him a lot," Max added.

Allison nodded.

"Look," he said. "Can we find some kind of way to help him?"

Allison thought about this proposal. "The book," she said. "The witches used it to put the spell on him. Maybe there's a way in here to take it off."

She dropped her sweater on Max's cluttered desk and walked back to the loft's staircase, where she plopped down on the bottom step.

"I don't know," said Max. "Binx told us not to open it."

Allison picked up the spell book. Every time she picked it up, it seemed to get heavier. "But the witches are dead," she said. "What harm could they do?"

Max nodded, thinking that over. "Well, just be careful."

"I will," Allison said, smirking. She undid the clasp that strapped the cover closed, then reached for Max's arm. "Hold my hand," she said.

He did, happily.

Allison took a breath and lifted the cover. She skimmed the first page, which included a list of names she assumed belonged to former owners of the book: Gunnilda Arden, Odelina Arden, Isolde Fitzrou, Mathilda Picardy, Eve and Amice and Frances Harvey, and then Cecily Sanderisson, Emma Sanderisone, Druscilla Sanderson, Winifred Sanderson, and last, Elizabeth Sanderson.

"That's odd," Allison said, examining the final name on the list. She ran a finger over it.

"What is?" Max asked.

"The last name on the list isn't Winifred's," she said. Shaking her head, she turned to the first page of spells. Max leaned forward to rest his chin on her shoulder. "Nothing here so far," she said, flipping to the next page.

Winifred Sanderson left the window of her childhood home and dragged her tired body to a fainting couch in the corner. This was the same chaise upon which her mother had birthed her and each of her sisters—quietly and all alone, as was a witch's way.

Mary and Sarah and even the two imprisoned boys watched as Winifred settled herself onto the fainting couch and began to weep into her hands and ash-streaked skirts. The sun would rise soon, and she'd expire in this small house alongside her hopeless sisters. And then what? The thought made Winifred sob even harder. She was afraid to go back to the place filled with fire and brimstone and catty witches—or worse, to go to no place at all. The idea of death chilled her to her marrow.

"Oh, Winnie," said Mary gently. "Do you want to hit me?"

She knelt and placed a hand on her sister's wrist. "Would that cheer you up?"

Winifred batted her hand away, and Mary sighed, straightening. She helped Winifred put her feet up. "There you go," she said, plucking up a fan and opening it to wash some fresh air over Winifred's face.

"This is the end," said Winifred. "I feel it."

"No," Mary said reassuringly, pumping the fan with more gusto.

But Winifred didn't believe her. No, Winifred knew that she would draw her last breath in the same house wherein she'd drawn her first.

"We are doomed," Winifred insisted. "I feel the icy breath of death upon my neck." The thought made her sick. She'd always been destined for more than these four walls. She'd been destined for greatness. Her tea leaves had always said so, which meant something, Winifred thought, even if she'd nudged the leaves around once or twice to properly decode them.

"Mary?" She looked around blearily, as if she couldn't see her sister right next to her. "Take me to the window. I wish to say good-bye." She struggled to rise, and Mary hurried to help her. "Good-bye. Good-bye, cruel world. Good-bye to life." Winifred reached the open window and leaned heavily on the sill.

Mary worried that not even the house's sturdy foundation could keep her sister on her feet.

"Good-bye to all that," Winifred said sadly.

As she did, she noticed something in the distance and straightened.

"Sister!" she said, reaching for Mary's arm. "Observe!"

Over the dark tree tops, near a full, heavy moon, shone a thin beam of reddish light.

"They opened it!" crowed Winifred, energy pumping back into her body. "Ha-ha! Just when our time was running out. Come! We fly!"

She dragged Mary to the closet. Sarah trailed behind them. Their own brooms were gone, leaving only a few objects meant for cleaning left by the humans who had turned their beloved house into a shop. Winifred, who was the first to look inside, snatched up the only broom. Sarah took the mop, holding her nose at the smell, and Mary fussed over the upright vacuum.

"What about us?" Ernie called after the witches' retreating backs.

Jay hushed him, but not before Sarah turned to them with a sultry, conniving smile.

"Oh, we'll have plenty of time for you," she said. She blew them a kiss as she followed her sisters through the front door.

Allison, who was becoming impatient with the number of spells in the huge book, turned to a new page.

"Oh, listen to this," she said, happy to have found anything useful at all. " 'Only a circle of salt can protect thy victims from thy power.' "

There was a yowl, and Binx leaped onto Max's lap and shoved the book shut. He climbed on top of it to keep Allison from reopening it, then hissed at Max and Allison in turn.

"We were just trying to help you," said Allison.

Binx batted at her shoulder. "Well, don't!" he said. "Nothing good can come from this book." He turned to swat at Max's face. "You got it?"

With that, he leaped down and padded back over to where Dani was sleeping.

Max looked apologetically at Allison. "Maybe we should go now," he said.

She hesitated before nodding. "Okay," she agreed, sounding disappointed. She set the book back on the loft's staircase and followed Max out of his room.

"Come on," he said. "I'll walk you home."

CHAPTER 11

AX PEERED into one of the other rooms accessible from the upstairs landing. "Mom?" he called. "Dad?" He turned back to Allison, shrugging. "They're still not home," he said. "That's weird. Must be having a great time."

"I dunno," Allison said, leading the way downstairs. "Something's not right. I'd feel a lot safer walking home if we had some salt."

Max led her into the narrow kitchen. The only window was set over a steel sink, and the cherry-patterned curtains were drawn back to let in a little moonlight. The space was clean but not yet unpacked: boxes were stacked, unopened, against one wall, and Max suspected they would be for a while.

"My mom's not much of a cook," he said apologetically, swinging open a set of white-painted cabinet doors and climbing onto one of the tiled counters to inspect the highest shelves.

"Sounds like my kind of lady," Allison joked. "When I'm an adult, the only thing I want to make are chocolate chip cookies."

"Milk or dark?" Max asked.

"Dark," said Allison, as if the answer were obvious.

"Oh, no way," said Max. "They're cookies. You gotta go milk."

Max found a spare canister of salt behind a bunch of sugar packets and spices that the previous homeowners had forgotten. He made a triumphant sound and tossed the paper cylinder to Allison. Then he dropped down to sit on the same counter she was leaning against.

Allison turned the container over in her hands, then paused and smirked.

"What's it say?" Max asked, leaning in. He noticed that Allison smelled like green apples and cinnamon.

Allison glanced at him, then back to the canister. "It says, 'Form a circle of salt to protect against zombies, witches, and old boyfriends.'"

"Yeah?" Max asked. "And what about new boyfriends?"

As she studied his face, Allison's lashes fluttered against the tops of her cheeks. Max noticed the quirk of a smile around the corners of her mouth, so he leaned forward. He skimmed the dip of her lip right below her nose, and he felt his pulse kick up to a dangerous RPM.

A crash thundered down the stairs, and both Allison and Max pulled away and looked at the ceiling.

"Dani," Max breathed.

He jumped down from the counter just as Allison pushed off toward the stairs. On his way up, he checked his jeans for the reassuring weight of his dad's pocketknife.

"Dani!" Max called as they rounded the upstairs landing and barreled back into his bedroom.

Dani had pulled the covers over her head, her hair just poking out of the top.

Max exhaled with relief and tossed his coat on the floor.

"Max," Allison said. "The book is gone."

He walked toward the narrow staircase that led to the loft. Sure enough, the book had disappeared. Allison snatched his wrist. "I'm telling you," she said, "something's weird."

Max hurried over to his sleeping sister and yanked back the covers. "Dani, wake up," he said.

But it was not Dani in his bed.

Sarah Sanderson sat bolt upright, beaming. "Trick or treat!"

Allison shrieked and leaped away. Max backed toward the closet, but its plantation doors accordioned open.

Mary and Winifred Sanderson strode out, both grinning. Winifred clutched the spell book, its patchwork front cover facing him. Mary had one hand around Dani's mouth and another around a large knitted sack.

"Looking for this?" Winifred demanded, waving her book.

"Or this?" Mary asked, tightening her fingers around Dani's face.

Max looked from Dani to the book and realized Binx was right: the spell book was dangerous, and it must've somehow betrayed them. Even as he thought this, the strange pucker of skin on its cover shivered a little and then opened, blinking blearily. It was an eye, and by the looks of it, the thing had been cut from a person's face.

Max shouted with disgust, stumbling away. Winifred raised her free hand and hit him with a bolt of white lightning. Max flew into the air and crashed into his drum set. Cymbals and drums went everywhere as he collapsed.

Allison popped the salt open and began to shake it wildly around the room.

"Salt!" said Winifred. "Ha! What a clever little white witch."

Allison brandished the container at her.

"But it will not save thy friends," Winifred continued. "No. Come, sisters." She plucked up her skirts and started up the stairs to the loft. "The candle's magic is almost spent. Dawn approaches."

Mary followed her, still clutching a struggling Dani. Sarah trailed after them both, looking from Max's prone body to Allison. She gave the girl a dark look, then stuck out her tongue and hurried after her sisters.

Dani bit down hard on Mary's finger. "Let me go!" she shouted when the witch had freed her mouth. "Put me down!"

Winifred launched lightning at the loft's small window, and the wall exploded in a shower of sparks and smoke that turned from pink to green to gray. The blast knocked Allison off her feet and sent a cascade of wood boards down the stairs.

Allison pushed herself back up and dashed for the stairs to the loft. "Dani!" she called between coughs. But the witches had flown away, and they'd taken both the spell book and Max's little sister with them.

Allison turned back to Max and shoved the snare drum off his chest. "Max, are you okay?" She helped him sit up.

He blinked groggily. "Where's Dani?"

Winifred gave a joyful shout as she led her sisters across the night sky, the three of them soaring high above Salem. The world below was full of so much more light than when she'd last been alive, including a slender lighthouse north of town that emitted a steady revolving beam. And yet it felt familiar and wonderful to have wind whipping through her curls and over her ankles and to have the smell of salt and frightened children in her lungs.

"Use thy voice, Sarah," Winifred called over her shoulder. "Fill the sky. Bring the little brats to die!"

Sarah peeled off then, veering down so her words would carry to prepubescent ears. Even from her height, though, Winifred could hear the sweet strains of Sarah's voice:

Come, little children,
I'll take thee away
into a land of enchantment.
Come, little children;
the time's come to play
here in my garden of magic.

The song filled Winifred's mouth with the taste of her mother's maggot-apple pie. It was the treat she had always asked for on her birthday, both because she loved the sweet fruit and

the flaky crust and because she loved to watch her mother's hands powdered with flour as she crimped the edges and wove the top crust together with quick, practiced fingers, pressing the wormy creatures back into the sugary goo before they could wriggle their way out.

Winifred clutched Dani's small body tighter. "My mother could not live forever," she whispered into the girl's ear. "But I'll make sure her rightful daughters do."

Dani squirmed and whined like a maggot herself, but Winifred's heart was full and warm and her teeth were ready for the crunch of crystallized sugar on a buttery crust, or for the roasted knuckle-bones of a towheaded girl—whichever Mary wanted to prepare first.

Max and Allison picked their way into the loft and looked out over Salem's dark streets. It was nearly six in the morning, but kids were out in hordes, some of them holding candles and others carrying flashlights and some empty-handed. A few of them were still in costumes, though the majority wore pajamas and night-gowns. All of them walked as if transfixed. They headed south in a silent, shuffling crowd.

"They're going to the Sanderson house," Allison said,

watching the scattered throng snake up the road and out of sight.

"Hey!" Max shouted down to the sleepwalking children.

Allison grabbed his arm. "It won't work," she said.

"Hey!" he yelled again, ignoring her. "Don't listen to them!" But just as with the adults at the Pumpkin Ball, nothing seemed to get their attention.

Allison shook him. "Max," she said. "Max, I figured it out. Winifred said 'The candle's magic will soon be spent, and dawn approaches.' The Black Flame Candle only brought them back for this one Halloween night—and unless they can steal the lives of children, when the sun comes up, they're dust."

"Yeah," Max said, turning to her, "but how can we make the sun come up? And they've got Dani. We need a miracle."

Allison gave him a helpless look. She looked back at the road and the flickering warmth of candles and flashlights dotting the eerie scene.

"I have an idea," she said. "Can you drive?"

The candles in the Sanderson house flickered low, and their yellowed wax softened and dripped down iron holders and wooden furniture in slow, slick rivulets.

"Can you pick the lock?" Jay asked Ernie.

"My kit's at home, man," said Ernie. He looked across the room at his friend. "Jay," he said, "I'm scared."

Jay was scared, too, but he knew he couldn't admit it. He was two months older than Ernie, and he was supposed to look out for him. So he said, "I won't let those hags eat you, Ern." *They might eat me, though,* he thought. But if they didn't, he'd be a better person. No more creeping on girls, no more breaking things that didn't belong to him, and no more stealing chips from the gas station. That last bit had always made him feel bad, anyway. His parents ran a small business, too—the groundskeeping service for the historical lighthouse on Winter Island—and he knew how tough it could be to get by.

The boys groaned in unison when Winifred and Mary Sanderson returned, this time with Max Dennison's mouthy little sister in tow.

Mary spent several minutes tying Dani to a chair before turning to the caged boys with a conniving grin. Winifred, meanwhile, opened her massive spell book and got to work. With a spark from her fingers, the fire beneath the cauldron leaped back to life.

Jay and Ernie protested as Mary pressed chocolate bars and gummy worms between the bars of their cages.

"No more candy," said Jay weakly.

"But we've got to fatten you up," said Mary.

"We should first eat the girl," said Winifred, almost absently, as she leaned closer to the simmering potion she'd been preparing for half an hour. "Otherwise, she'll start to spoil."

She and Mary and Dani looked up when the weathered front door creaked open. Jay and Ernie looked, too, though both boys moved sluggishly, as if they'd long before given up hope of getting free.

Sarah entered, her purple cloak billowing dramatically around her narrow body. "The children," she said, beaming, "are coming."

Winifred clapped. "Well done, Sister Sarah!"

Dani tugged harder on her rope bindings, but it only seemed to tighten them.

Behind her, she heard Binx wriggling in the woolen sack that Mary had strung from the mantle. He yowled, and his claws scratched at the thick fabric. "Let me out of here," he demanded.

"If I did, thou wouldst drop into the fire," chided Mary.

"She's doing you a favor," Sarah agreed, pausing near the sack to give it a light pat where she thought Binx's head might be. He struck out at her hand, but it only prompted a giggle from her currant-colored lips. The burlap caught Binx's claws and trapped them. As he struggled to rescue his paw, Sarah leaned in closer. "Sweet kitty," she cooed. Her nose nearly touched the burlap.

"You'll make a good roast." She giggled again and turned away.

Winifred finished tending the bubbling cauldron and moved instead to her book, which she'd returned to its ornate wooden stand.

"Soon the lives of all thy little friends will be mine," she told Dani, "and I shall be young and beautiful again forever."

"It doesn't matter how young or old you are!" Dani spat back. "You sold your soul. You're the ugliest thing that's ever lived, and you know it."

Winifred gave her a long, cold look. "You'll die first," she said crisply. She stalked back to the cauldron and bit off a chunk of her own tongue, spitting it into the potion while eyeing Dani. The liquid's surface erupted with huge, hungry bubbles. Behind her, Ernie and Jay groaned.

Dani's ears pricked at the crunch of tires on gravel. It was their parents' big car: she recognized the deep purr of the motor from many weekends spent lying awake waiting for her parents to come back from friends' dinner parties. The thought made her remember those Saturday evenings with Max, when he'd order a pizza and help her with homework before starting his own. Sometimes he'd even give in when she begged him to watch *Rescue Rangers* or *DuckTales* with her instead of practicing his drums.

Dani glanced at the Sanderson witches, but none of them seemed to hear the sound. Max was there to save her, she knew, and after he did, she'd never make him watch cartoons with her again unless she thought he secretly wanted to.

Winifred gave a delighted yelp, snapping Dani's attention back to the horrors at hand. "'Tis ready," the eldest witch said, giving the potion a final stir. "Pry open her mouth."

"Dani, don't drink it!" Binx called from his cloth prison.

"Shut up, you," said Winifred. She scooped up some of the bubbling liquid in her huge spoon.

Sarah hurried over to Dani and pinched her jaw. Her fingers were surprisingly strong, but Dani kept her teeth tightly clenched.

"Dani!" Binx shouted, unable to see what was happening. "Don't drink it, Dani!"

Mary went over to help her sisters. She forced a thumb between Dani's lips, then sprang back. "Ow!" she shouted. "She bit me!"

Dani brought her foot down hard on Sarah's toes.

Though both of her sisters were incapacitated, Winifred still advanced with her spoon.

The door flew open, crashing into the wall. "Prepare to die!" shouted Max. "Again."

"Hollywood," Jay said, jutting his chin at his cage's padlock.

Winifred turned to Max. "You," she said, splashing some of

her potion in the process. It sizzled against the floorboards. "You have no powers here, you fool." She refocused her attention on Dani.

Meanwhile, Sarah had regained her footing and tried once more to force open Dani's mouth. Dani shook her head hard and squirmed, trying to protect her face from the witch's sharp nails. Winifred pressed the spoon against her mouth, putting it as close to the girl's nose as she could in the hopes that the putrid smell would force her to gasp or breathe through her mouth, swallowing the potent liquid in the process.

"Maybe not," Max said to Winifred. "But there's a power greater than your magic, and that's knowledge. And there's one thing I know that you don't."

Winifred, frustrated, pulled the spoon away from Dani and whirled on Max. "And what is that, *dude?*"

Her sisters chortled like ravens.

"Daylight savings time," he said.

Mary parroted the strange phrase, mocking his accent. Sarah snorted.

The orange light of sunrise pierced the eastern windows of the house, shining warm and rosy and sure through the glass.

The witches shrank back.

"Max, get me out of here," Dani said desperately.

At once, the Sanderson sisters collapsed onto the floor, writhing in pain.

"It hurts!" Sarah shrieked.

Max ran over and cut Dani's ties with his dad's pocketknife. Once freed, Dani jumped up and ran to the fireplace to save Binx.

"Hey!" cried Jay. "Let me out of here! Help!"

Max unhooked the bag containing Binx and handed it to Dani. "Get outside," he said with a push to her shoulder.

The witches continued to whimper underfoot. Winifred pulled her cloak over her face and hands to protect her skin.

"Hey, Hollywood!" said Ernie.

Max strode over and examined the bully, whose legs were dangling out of the cage.

"Help us out here?" Ernie asked.

Max pulled his stolen shoes from Ernie's feet. "Tubular," he said, holding the Nikes up in salute. On his way to the door, he pushed over the cauldron, spilling the soul-sucking potion over the floor. It bubbled and smoked and spilled through the spaces between the floorboards as Winifred wailed.

"Let me outta here, man," Jay pleaded.

"Come on, Dani," Max said, taking Binx from her since she was struggling with the sack. "Let's go."

As they stepped out of the house, Dani stopped. "Max, I want to see her turn to dust," she said.

Just then, she spotted her mom's gray SUV. Allison was standing next to it, gesturing desperately at the headlights, which were covered in a colored film that turned their light orange.

"Pump it!" Dani yelled, running for the car.

Max followed her, ripping the cellophane from the headlights as he passed them.

He jumped into the driver's seat, pushed Binx into Allison's arms, and revved the engine.

The dawn thinned and vanished with a roar and a rumble.

CHAPTER 12

ARAH ROLLED onto her back and stared at the high ceiling of the house she'd been born in. Firelight flickered over the sturdy roof beams, highlighting swathes of cobwebs and colonies of spiders. She went through a mental checklist from the roots of her hair to the nails of her toes. Her hip hurt a little, but then again she had fallen on it in her hurry to avoid the burning glint of sunrise. Everything else felt fine.

"I'm alive," she said, smiling.

"Damn that boy!" said Winifred, who'd collapsed first and now lay beneath both Sarah and Mary. "He's tricked us again." She got clumsily to her feet. Her face was as red as her hair.

"Oh, you're right," said Mary, shifting uncomfortably beneath Sarah's weight. "You're always right. I don't know how you do that."

"It's my curse," said Winifred to Mary. "That, and you two. Get off me, you thundering oafs!"

Sarah sprang up, dusted off her skirts, and pulled her lucky rat tail from her sleeve. Chewing it always made her feel better, especially when Winifred was out of sorts.

Mary and Winifred scrambled up after her.

"Look," said Winifred. She crossed to the kitchen, where the Black Flame Candle waited on a cluttered counter, its mysterious flame diminished to a weak flicker. The scene on the outside of the candle had all but melted away, and the taper was reduced to a runny stub. "The candle is almost out," she said, then gained the courage to turn and examine the fallen cauldron and the puddled floorboards. "And my potion. My beautiful potion." She knelt by the cauldron, not caring that the cooling liquid soaked her clothes. "Look," she said. She knelt down even lower and peered into the depths of the pot. "There's just enough left for one child."

The room seemed to grow very quiet, and the silence made Jay and Ernie even more conspicuous. They were biting their lips and staring at each other, each wordlessly threatening mortal harm if the other made a sound.

Winifred turned to Mary. "Get the vial," she said.

Sarah took her a glass bottle whose base was wide and round

and whose neck was long and thin. Carefully, Winifred ladled the last of the potion into the bottle. She pressed the cork back into its mouth and clutched the treasure to her chest.

"What luck," she said, smiling. She turned to the door through which Max and Dani had escaped only minutes before, and her voice grew sharp: "This is perfect for that little towheaded brat."

"We have a child," said Sarah, gesturing at the two hanging cages.

Jay and Ernie each pointed at the other, shouting "Him!"

Mary, for her part, leaned against the front window and watched the yard with dreamy interest. "And look, Winnie: more children are arriving." She beckoned to the sleepwalkers. "Come on in," she cooed.

"Winnie," Sarah said, touching her sister's forearm, "we'll make more potion because we have the book." She pointed to the spell book, which still lay open on the pedestal.

"We haven't the time," said Winifred. "Besides, I want to get that little rat-faced kid that called me—"

"Oh," Mary said, rushing over, "don't say it."

"Ugly?" asked Sarah.

Winifred and Mary both cringed.

"She really hurt my feelings," whimpered Winifred. "She doesn't even know me." She took Sarah's outstretched hand and dried her eyes on it. "You know," she said, composing herself, "I always wanted a child, and now I think I'll have one. On toast!"

Dani sat in the back of her parents' car, clutching Binx in her lap. Max was driving, which made her even more scared because his last practice session had ended in a long argument with their dad about what constituted a rolling stop.

"There are too many kids," Max said, careening around another group of transfixed children. He recognized a few of them from Dani's class and felt a pang of worry. He leaned out his window. "Go home!" he shouted, but of course they didn't listen to him. They didn't even seem to hear him. Max groaned and pounded the steering wheel. "We need to wait in the cemetery until sunrise," he said. "But these zombie kids are going to trap us on the road."

"Try that side road." Allison pointed off to the left, back into the woods. "It'll reconnect to the main road in town, and you can circle around to the front of the cemetery."

Max nodded. He knew it was a risk since it would take longer, but he also knew that it would put them closer to the clearing Binx had shown them before. From there, it would be easier to see the witches coming—and to go back into the sewers if needed.

Before any other kids blocked their way, Max veered to the left as Allison suggested and headed deeper into the trees. He clenched his sweaty fists tighter around the steering wheel as visions of careening off the road swam through his head. The engine growled as he goaded the accelerator.

The sprinklers, the kiln, the fake sunrise—how many times could they trick the witches before their tricks didn't work any longer? Max realized their time was running out—but so was the Sanderson sisters'. If Allison was right, they just had to keep them at bay until sunrise.

If Allison was right.

Max glanced at her. "Are they following us?" he asked.

Allison turned around in her seat. "No," she said.

Max smiled. "Good."

Just then, Winifred Sanderson appeared at the driver's side window, her body angled forward against the handle of her broom.

Max swerved away but kept going; Allison reached over to steady the steering wheel and help ease them back toward the middle of the road before they skidded off of it.

"Pull over," Winifred demanded. "Let me see your driver's license."

Max considered sticking his arm out the window to push her away, but that seemed like a terrible idea on several fronts. Instead, he gripped the wheel even tighter and banked the car to the left, knocking her and her broom out of the way. He grinned again, but this time he wiped his palms—one and then the other—on his jeans.

"We're gonna be okay," Allison told him. He nodded tightly and pressed on, taking a sharp turn onto the street that held the graveyard entrance facing downtown Salem.

He slammed on the breaks in the middle of the street and hopped out, not bothering to take the keys with him. Allison helped Dani and Binx out of the back seat before grabbing a packed duffel bag from the floor. The group hurried through the gate, breathing more easily once they were safe on hallowed ground—that is, until Max slammed into Billy Butcherson.

Dani shrieked and Allison hurried back to help him, but Max shouted at them to go. Then he pulled out his dad's pocketknife.

The girls were gone when Winifred arrived a second later, still clutching her broom. She floated near the top of the gate and shouted down at Billy, who was fighting Max for the knife.

"Catch the children!" she said.

Max winced as Billy overpowered him, forcing the knife closer and closer to Max's throat. Then Billy surprised him by levering Max's hand higher, above his head. Billy sliced through the threads that sewed his mouth shut. He released Max then and gave a dry, guttural cough. Small brown moths flew from his lips and fluttered away.

"Come now," Winifred ordered. "Kill him. Do it now!"

"Wench," Billy snapped at Winifred. "Trollop!" Max found this a bit rich since Billy had been the one running around with his girlfriend's younger sister. "You bucktoothed, mop-riding fire-fly from Hell."

Winifred let out a scandalized screech.

"I've waited centuries to say that," Billy told Max.

"Say what you want," Max said, shrinking away. "Just don't breathe on me."

"Billy," said Winifred. "I killed you once, I shall kill you again, you maggoty malfeasance."

Billy grabbed Max around the waist and tugged, pulling both of them into the woods.

"Hang on to your heads!" Winifred called after them.

Her taunt followed them, but she didn't bother flying over the graveyard gate, which worried Max. The witches had to be plotting something.

It didn't take long for Max and Billy to find Allison and Dani in the clearing that housed Billy's open grave—which meant, Max feared, that it wouldn't take long for the witches to find them, either.

Allison and Dani scrambled up, each holding a sturdy branch.

"Max, run!" shouted Dani.

"Max, move out of the way," said Allison, charging.

Max threw himself between her and Billy. "Wait!" he said. "No. No, no. He's a good zombie."

Allison gave the dead man a searching look.

"You're sure?" she asked Max. "How do I know you're not just saying that because you've been bitten?"

Max gave her a look, and Allison relented. "Okay, fine."

Billy followed the pair down the low hill, toward both Dani and his own open grave.

"Hi, Billy!" Dani said, waving.

Max looked at her face: her fear was gone, and she seemed to think the idea of befriending a zombie was totally reasonable. Was she so adaptable because she was still a kid? He couldn't remember ever being like that. Maybe she really did have a thing or two to teach him. He hoped they'd all survive the night so she could.

Billy helped Dani into his grave. "You'll be safe in here," he said.

Max dug through their duffel bag of supplies. He handed Allison a fresh carton of salt and pulled out a baseball bat for himself.

"You okay, Dani?" he asked his sister.

"Yeah," she said in a small voice. "I'm fine."

Adaptable or not, she was still his sister, and they both knew she was still in danger. He adjusted his grip on the bat and practiced swinging a few times.

Allison opened the salt container and drew a circle of it around the grave.

"Here they come," said Binx, who was perched on a headstone. "Billy, guard Dani. Max, Allison: spread out."

They'd just taken their places when Winifred descended from

the dark sky. Her dress and robes fluttered around her, caught by a light autumn wind.

"For the last time," she said, "prepare to meet thy doom."

She swooped low, heading for Dani. Max took a swing at her with the baseball bat.

Winifred veered to the side, cackling, and then course-corrected. This time, she bore down on Max. "You little pest," she said to him. "I've had enough of you."

He swung at her again, but Winifred grabbed the bat from his hands and flung it away, chortling.

Max made to run then, but Winifred was a step ahead. She opened her palm, and a branch of electricity rippled out of her skin and made contact with the nearest tree, right at the joint between its trunk and heaviest branch. Dani screamed as the branch toppled down, blocking Max's path and separating him from his friends.

Billy, who stood between Dani and the witch, glowered at Winifred. "Go to Hell!" he said.

The eldest Sanderson smiled tightly. "Oh, I've already been there, thank you," she said. "I found it quite lovely."

CHAPTER 13

ARAH AND MARY—the first on a ratty mop and the second on an upright vacuum—dove toward Max and Allison. Max fled to the right and Allison to the left, splitting up the two witches as they scrambled into the woods and tried to seek shelter among the trees.

Winifred cackled, pleased that her sisters had followed her instructions for once. Billy took a step closer to her. He looked as if he was going to say something else spiteful, but Winifred gave another sharp laugh before diving straight toward him. Dani, hidden in the open grave, gave a frightened warning shout. Billy lifted his arms to grab for Winifred's broom handle, but he missed. Winifred pulled up at the last moment and thrust her legs forward, kicking him in the jaw. His head flew off for the second time that night and bounced and rolled to a stop several feet away.

In the woods, Allison slipped behind a huge pine tree as Sarah turned a corner, and waited there until she was sure she was safe. After a few heart-stopping seconds of ducking and weaving, Max dove under a half-collapsed tree and waited in the leaves until Mary swept past, calling out "Sister Sarah! I lost our dinner!"

From her safe spot in Billy's grave, Dani peeked out from between her fingers. When Winifred left to track down her sisters, who were weaving through the woods calling for Allison and Max, Dani dragged herself out of the grave and hurried over to rescue Billy's head.

Max and Allison stumbled out of the woods at the same time and spotted each other from across the clearing. Max lifted his chin in recognition, then headed straight for Billy Butcherson's grave. He froze so suddenly Allison almost crashed into him from behind. Dani had disappeared.

Allison spotted Dani first and tugged on Max's sleeve. The youngest Dennison was several yards away. She'd gingerly picked up Billy's head and was offering it to his body, which was desperately shuffling through leaves and sticks. "I think you dropped this," she said.

As Billy reattached his head, everyone heard a familiar shout.

Winifred reemerged from the woods, her sisters at her heels. She aimed her broom handle toward Dani and Billy, and before Max could run or shout or even blink, Winifred had his little sister around the middle and was lifting her into the sky.

Billy, Max, and Allison took off after them, while Binx watched helplessly from where he stood before a gravestone.

"Bye-bye, big brother," called Winifred over her shoulder. She pulled from her robes a glass bulb filled with green liquid. Then she looked at Dani and gritted her teeth. "All right, you little trollimog."

Sarah and Mary waited some distance away, celebrating their sister's success by spinning in wide circles on their mop and vacuum, fingers barely touching.

"Hold on, Dani!" called Binx, dashing over rocks and gravestones in her direction.

Winifred bit down on the bottle's cork and yanked it from the neck of the bottle. She spat it onto the ground. "This will teach you to call people ugly," she said. "Open your mouth."

Binx ran up the sturdy branch Winifred had torn down only minutes before. He leaped from its highest point and knocked the vial from her hand. As Winifred reached for it, he clawed at her face and arms until she flung him away. Binx gave a yowl as he hit the ground, but he was on his feet in a moment and scrambling to shelter in the underbrush.

The potion bottle tumbled end over end as it fell, but somehow not a drop of liquid spilled. Max caught the bottle. White smoke bubbled out of the top, smelling of saltwater taffy and pond scum.

"Give me that vial," said Winifred.

Max held it over his head. "Put her down, or I'll smash it."

"Smash it," said Winifred, "and she dies."

Allison called his name and tried to run over to him, but Billy pulled her back.

"He's got a plan," Billy whispered to her. "I think."

Max glared at Winifred. She said she would kill his sister if he broke the bottle, but he knew that if he handed it over she'd just kill her anyway, slowly sucking out Dani's life force in front of him, just like Binx had told him they had done to his poor sister Emily. He couldn't be the one to sentence his own sister to that.

But he could do it to himself.

He lifted the bottle to his lips and took a long swig, swallowing the whole thing. It bubbled and burned as it went down his throat.

"Max, no!" shouted Dani.

But it was too late.

Sarah and Mary froze, shocked by the turn of events. They waited for Winifred's reaction.

Winifred gasped, recoiling as if she'd been burned.

Max smashed the empty bottle against a nearby tombstone and glared up at the eldest Sanderson. "Now you have no choice," he said. "You have to take me."

Winifred descended slowly. "What a fool you are, to give up thy life for thy sister's."

When Mary and Sarah heard Winifred's words, the two of them exchanged a look.

As she neared the ground, Winifred released Dani and grabbed Max's collar instead.

Dani collapsed, sobbing, and Billy and Allison hurried to help her up.

Winifred, who was surprisingly strong, lifted Max by only his shirt. His body had begun to glow, letting off a golden, pearlescent sheen that moved when he moved, but at a more leisurely rate.

Winifred brought Max's face close to hers and opened her mouth. A narrow stream of light peeled off from the rest of him and coursed past her lips and down her throat. Max's eyes grew wide, for he could feel the draining sensation somewhere in his chest. He felt, also, like he was growing older, as if each second were a lost year. The world suddenly wasn't so funny anymore.

Distantly, he could hear Allison and Dani screaming, but he didn't know what to do about it. For some reason, all he could think of was the red plastic car he'd gotten for his fourth or fifth birthday. He'd raced around in it, pedaling the thing with his feet like a Flintstone and shouting that he'd be a race car driver one day. Then he thought of the day Dani had been born, and how his father had put the small squirming pink thing in his arms and told him that now he had responsibilities, and he'd looked at his baby sister and felt a warm, comfortable weight settle around his shoulders. He thought of meeting Jack, and of hearing the Ramones for the first time, and of screaming at his parents when

they sat him down and explained that his dad had taken a job on the East Coast, in Salem, Massachusetts. And then he thought of Allison and her vases and her laugh and their conversation in the sewers, when she'd told him she liked him better when he was around Dani, and how he'd realized that maybe he liked himself better then, too.

Max reached up and pushed Winifred's face away. She swatted his hand at first, but he tried again, with as much force as he could muster. As she turned her face away and had to close her mouth, the remainder of Max's life force coalesced back around his body. Having it closer to his skin made him feel more solid—and more aware of his surroundings. This gave Max an idea, and he heaved his whole body toward Winifred, scrabbling for her throat and digging his thumbs into the hollow of it. The witch gagged and pushed back at him, finally shoving him hard enough that he almost fell. He was left clinging to the handle of her broom by only his fingers.

Max pulled down hard, flipping the broom, and suddenly Winifred was unseated and hanging by only her fingers, too, scrambling to get a better hold on the prickly bristles. "Hallowed ground!" she said desperately, looking down. "Hallowed ground! Sisters!"

"Winnie!" called Mary. "I'm coming!"

The brunet witch sailed over the other children, not realizing that her vacuum cleaner's cord was dangling within their reach. Dani grabbed it by the plug and dug her heels into the soft earth. Allison and Billy anchored themselves to the cord, too. Mary only made it a few more feet before the cord stopped her from

going any farther. She looked over her shoulder and let out a strangled cry when she realized what had gone wrong. That only made Allison, Billy, and Dani pull harder on the line.

"I'm going to teach you a lesson you'll never forget," Winifred said to Max as they both struggled to pull themselves back onto the broom. They spun and spun like a top as, in the east, a sliver of orange light broke the horizon. Winifred pulled herself back onto the broom, but the promise of sunrise gave Max a second burst of energy. He just had to wait for it to reach his tingling fingers.

"Sarah!" Mary pleaded, still struggling against the spiteful humans trying to drag her onto the graveyard soil. Beneath her, the vacuum revved and whined.

Sarah flew down and grasped her sister's hand, tugging, but Billy, Allison, and Dani had better leverage. With each tug, they pulled Mary a little closer to the ground.

"Let go—now!" shouted Allison. They all did at once, and the released tension sent Mary and Sarah spinning through the air.

Winifred watched her sisters arc over the treetops, trying desperately to right themselves, so she didn't notice when Max swung his body around and put all his weight into knocking her from her place on the broom.

She hit the ground with a heavy thud. Max dropped down a few feet away, panting. Winifred roared as she turned over and began to crawl toward him. Her movements were stiff and labored, though, as if each additional pull of muscle and twist of tendon was more and more difficult to control. Her long nails, as sharp and hooked as claws, dug into the earth each time she planted her hands, and each time she pulled them back, earth and grass flew up and muddied her palms and wrists.

Max pushed himself away from her, but he was so, so tired. Gold light shimmered before his eyes.

At last, Winifred grabbed him by the front of his sweater and lifted him up, struggling with her own aching hips as she stood. She opened her mouth to suck the life from him, but when Max looked down he saw that the curled toes of her boots had begun to smoke and harden into granite.

The stone crackled over her skin from the soles of her feet to her calves and knees and stomach and shoulders and head, until Max found himself dangling from the grasping fingers of a furious statue.

He wiggled about, ripping himself free. He grunted when he hit the ground, but the gold halo surrounding his body faded as the sun fully broke over Salem Harbor. A scrap of his shirt hung from Winifred's stone talons, fluttering meekly like a flag of surrender.

Above the graveyard, Sarah gave a squeak before bursting into a cloud of purple glitter. Mary's jaw dropped open just as she

exploded in a firework of red smoke. Their mop and vacuum hit the ground with two distinct thuds.

Winifred's statue began to quiver and then crack, and with a burst it blew apart, lighting up the world, briefly, with a lime-green glow.

Max sucked in a disbelieving breath and collapsed onto his back. For a moment, his entire world consisted of his pattering heart, the sweet relief swimming through his head, and morning's gray light.

CHAPTER 14

AX, FROM his place on the ground, buried his face in both arms.

"Max?" called a tentative voice, but he was still dazed and didn't know how to answer. Instead, he heaved himself into a sitting position and looked around at the clearing, where nothing had changed and everything had changed. The witches were gone, but there had been witches. He was alive, but he'd nearly had his essence drained out through his pores. And Dani—

"Dani!" he said, turning to try to find his sister.

She was dashing down the low hill toward him.

"Max," she said, kneeling beside him. He thought he'd never heard her sound quite so gentle. "Are you okay?"

"Yeah," he croaked. "I think so."

"You saved my life," she said.

He looked at her small surprised face. "Well, I had to. I'm your big brother."

She beamed. "I love you, jerk face," she said.

"I love you, too."

She threw her arms around his neck, and he wrapped one of his own around her back.

"Come on," Dani said after a few seconds. She helped him to his feet and led him to Billy's grave. Winifred's ex was already climbing back into his broken coffin.

Allison walked over and slipped an arm around Max's shoulders. She felt solid and stable and *real* in a way that still seemed to escape the rest of the graveyard—and even Dani, who was helping Billy get settled in his coffin.

Max wound his free arm around Allison's waist.

"It all really happened, didn't it?" he asked her.

She squeezed his arm. "Yeah," she said.

The Black Flame Candle, the Sanderson sisters, his almost kiss with Allison in his parents' still packed kitchen. Binx and Billy and Dani's kidnap and rescue, and Max's own life drifting into a witch's angry mouth before his eyes. All of it was real.

Despite how unbelievable the night had been, Allison made him feel grounded just by standing near him. In fact, having Allison so close made Max think that he could take on the world, at least if he was with her. He looked back at the broken remains of Winifred's statue and realized that maybe they already had. And maybe they would have to again, but it wouldn't be so scary the second time around.

"Bye, Billy," Dani said as he reached for his coffin's lid. "Have a nice sleep."

"Hey, Billy," called Max.

Billy Butcherson paused and gave Max an expectant look.

"Thanks," Max said.

Allison waved good-bye with a small smile on her face.

Billy waved in return, then stretched his whole body with a big yawn and dropped back into the remains of his bed.

Dani looked around. "Binx," she said. "Where's Binx?"

She broke away from Max to track down the cat, but what she found brought her to her knees.

"No . . ." she said, gasping. Binx's body lay still and lifeless at the foot of a leafless tree.

"He's gone, Dani," Allison said softly.

"But he can't die, remember?" Dani touched his narrow shoulder. "Binx," she said. "Binx, wake up. Like last time."

When he didn't move, she broke into a fresh wave of sobbing.

"Come on," said Binx's voice, though it wasn't coming from the cat. "Please don't be sad for me."

Allison, Max, and Dani all looked around.

A few feet away stood a young man—likely Max's age—wearing a billowing white tunic that was open at the collar. The warm light of daybreak filtered through his skin and clothes as if he wasn't entirely there.

"Binx, is that you?" Dani asked.

"Yeah," said the ghost. His dark blond hair was pulled back and tied in a short tail, and he was smiling. "The witches are dead. My soul's finally free."

Dani took a step toward him.

"You freed me, Dani," Binx said. "Thank you." He looked from her to her brother. "Hey, Max," he added. "Thanks for lighting the candle."

Max snorted. "Any time."

"Thackery?" The asker was a semitranslucent little girl in a white dress and white cap. She peered around the trunk of a tall tree. "Thackery Binx?" she called.

"It's Emily," said Binx, looking back at his new friends and smiling. He leaned down and gave Dani a kiss on the cheek. "I shall always be with you," he whispered.

Dani nodded, and with that Binx took off and joined his little sister, hugging her and then taking her hand.

"Thackery Binx, what took you so long?" she asked, gazing up at him.

"I'm sorry, Emily," he said. The pair walked off toward the sunrise in the direction of the large iron gates to the cemetery. "I had to wait three hundred years for a virgin to light a candle."

As Max, Allison, and Dani watched them go, Max placed a hand on Dani's shoulder and pulled her a little closer to him. He'd never forget Binx's caution to look after her.

The figures of Thackery and Emily dissolved into light and shadow and a trick of the sun through autumn leaves, and Max crouched to give Dani a hug.

She giggled before pushing him away.

"So," said Allison, bumping Max with her hip. "Did I make a believer out of you?"

They both laughed. "Yeah," said Max. "I guess so."

It was hard to tell who started the kiss or how long it lasted, but as soon as they came up for air they dove back in, Max cupping Allison's face in both of his hands and Allison pulling him closer by the hem of his sweater.

Dani gave them a few seconds of privacy before clearing her throat loudly. "Can we go home?" she asked. "I'm tired, and I haven't gotten a single piece of candy tonight."

Max laughed and pushed her ahead of him as they all headed back to the family car.

"Sure thing, kid," he said.

"I'm glad you saved me, Max," said Dani, as if she'd actually been debating the pros and cons. "Now I get to bug you for years and years."

Allison laughed hard at that, which made Dani laugh, too.

Max knitted his fingers through Allison's as they followed Dani to the graveyard gate. "Can't wait," he said.

And he meant it.

THE END